# Double-Barrelled

The money, the looks, the brains . . . rich banker Abdon Timpson has it all – and he knows it. But his uppity arrogance doesn't help Abdon when the sheriff cuffs him and locks him up for the night. There's a gunman on the loose, and this outlaw is a dead ringer for Abdon. The shootings don't stop when Abdon's in jail, though, and it looks like Abdon's folks have been hiding something from him. Abdon learns a thing or two about himself – and it isn't pretty.

*By the same author*

Texan Secrets
Vulture Wings

# Double-Barrelled

Dirk Hawkman

A Black Horse Western

ROBERT HALE

First published in Great Britain 2019

ISBN 978-0-7198-2949-9

The Crowood Press
The Stable Block
Crowood Lane
Ramsbury
Marlborough
Wiltshire SN8 2HR

www.bhwesterns.com

Robert Hale is an imprint
of The Crowood Press



*For Carys*

Typeset by
Derek Doyle & Associates, Shaw Heath
Printed and bound in Great Britain by
4Bind Ltd, Stevenage, SG1 2XT

# PROLOGUE

The little girl screamed in agony. So piercing were her anguished cries that the back of her gorge was raw.

Her name was Zofia, or something like that. Calista did not know for certain, nor care. Young Zofia was going to make Calista a lot of money. That was all that mattered to her.

Zofia was far too young to be wed, but old enough to conceive. Though Calista could not quite place her age, she seemed very young indeed. They usually were, Calista remarked. The agonies of childbirth were only part of the torment. Calista's charges never seemed to know what was going to happen during birthing. Indeed, they normally had no idea where babies came from, despite their condition.

Zofia was a charming, pretty, blue-eyed blonde when Calista first met her. Presently, though, Zofia's eyes were screwed shut in pain. The girl's flesh had lost its colour and had turned sickly and ashen. Calista soaked a cloth in the dirty bowl sat on the cabinet beside Zofia's bed. The midwife wiped away the steaming perspiration from her patient's brow. In a thin pretence of compassion, Calista ran her fingers through Zofia's soaking golden locks. The sensation sickened the midwife, but she masked her disgust with a well-practised smile.

Zofia mumbled something in Polish. The girl barely spoke English. Calista did not understand the guttural ramblings. Zofia's incoherent words were punctuated by desperate gasps.

Calista gave her ward's brow another wipe. This Zofia was testing her patience. It had been a long, long night and Calista's energies were fading. She made a brief examination of the baby's progress.

'It won't be long, now, honey,' Calista reassured with as much sincerity as she could fake. 'Stay strong for Calista.'

The midwife looked over her patient. Zofia lay spread-eagled on the filthy bed Calista had furnished. The nurse rented the single-roomed cabin, discreetly distant from Cowbridge, for all of her deliveries. The shack was remote enough that the screams of Calista's protégés would not be carried too far. Indeed, Zofia's tormented shrieks had been particularly irksome to Calista tonight. The girl had also lost a great deal of blood. Though it was late October, the heat within the delivery room was dizzying.

'Time for a break,' Calista thought. While the cabin was poorly lit by the pale jaundice of cheap candles, the midwife could make out Zofia's fraught eyes imploring her as Calista stepped outside.

Without, it was biting cold, but the frigid air was a pleasing relief to the midwife. Starless, the sky was an empty black oblivion. Calista could scarcely make out her hand in front of her face, so dense was the gloom. On another night, this site in the countryside might have been peaceably silent. Tonight, though, the tranquillity was ruined by

Zofia's violent screams and queasy rasping.

Calista tried not to listen as she lit her cigar. As she puffed away, she permitted her mind to wander for a little while. Within a few minutes, Calista's thoughts were pleasantly elsewhere. She took her mind off the tiresome chore lying pathetically on the bed inside. The sharp winter air seemed to enhance the flavour of her smoke. She drew a slug of whiskey from her hip flask.

Zofia's family were Polish settlers ashamed of their progeny's sinfulness. Papists, they had convinced themselves that the baby should be adopted into a good home. Though she called herself a midwife, Calista was more of a businesswoman. Her clientele did not truly pay her for her medical skills; Calista's customers paid her to make a problem go away. Unfaithful wives, unwed mothers, girls a little too young to be in the family way, and sometimes even despairing Romeos: Calista could help – for the right price. She could arrange for the childbirth to be in secret, and then she could make that unwanted brat disappear.

Slim, young and flame-haired, Calista was very beautiful – yet stony and aloof. Utterly single-minded, she could switch from iciness to enchanting persuasiveness in an instant when she sensed an opportunity. Calista had contacts in orphanages around the territory, but sometimes she placed the babies with childless couples. She already had a buyer lined up for the golden egg that Zofia was about to lay.

Reluctantly exhaling her last puff, Calista ground out her cigar and returned inside. Skilfully faking a benign smile, she took another look at Zofia's birth canal.

'We're nearly there, honey. One last push.'

Calista urged her patient on with as much enthusiasm as

she could feign. The nurse lay a comforting hand on Zofia's. Calista was taken aback when the little girl grasped the midwife's fingers with an iron grip that belied her youth. Zofia's hand was slippery with perspiration, but her embrace was powerful. Calista was reminded of a steel mantrap when Zofia's jaws pressed together in torture. For a second, the nurse wondered if Zofia would snap her own teeth.

When the sound of a child's helpless bawling tore at the air, Calista felt relieved. It had been a trying night, but the midwife's watch was drawing to its conclusion. Calista attended to the umbilical cord, washed the wailing little creature, and lay it in a cradle she had brought with her. Calista hated to sully herself with the filth from Zofia's guts, but it was all part of the charade.

The midwife noted that Zofia had watched her ministrations with exhausted, yet longing, eyes. Her charge had also become silent. Calista resented that insolent stare. Zofia's response was brief, though, for she began to writhe and moan once more. It was as if the girl was entering labour again.

The nurse did not bother to hide her indignation when she brusquely spread Zofia's legs for another look. When Calista saw another baby crowning, she sighed in exasperation. The midwife's impatience was brief, though.

'Twins,' Calista thought to herself. 'This means big bucks.'

# CHAPTER 1

He was going to need to kill her quickly.

Late as it was, the old woman was still awake. It was near impossible to make out her wooden cabin in the winter gloom, but lamplight shone through the building's windows. The intruder lay flat on the grass, watching. He had tied his mount to a nearby tree. The horse's occasional snorts were the only sounds through the nocturnal hush. He shivered as the fields, coarsened by frost, drew the heat from his body. The burglar's fingers pulsed in the cold, but he willed them to stop. Tonight, he would have to make his bullets count.

Lizzie Adams lived all alone out on her homestead. The intruder had asked a couple of locals about her. He could be persuasive and outwardly friendly when he wanted. However, the interloper had been forced to be selective. His false charm was not the problem. The burglar had a disfigurement on his cheek, a birthmark as thick as a bloody scar. It was in the shape of a scythe. This was why he preferred to thieve and murder by night. His deformity made him all too memorable to witnesses.

The burglar rose to his feet, but remained hunched

down, his knees bent. He drew the revolver from his holster. In the frigid air, the gunmetal was so icy that it felt almost painful in his palm. He tried to creep silently as he approached the little house, but his feet crunched on the solidified grass. So hushed was the night air that he could hear his own nervous breathing. The footpad was skilled in picking locks, writhing through windows, and stealth. Tonight would be no ordinary housebreak, though. He wanted Lizzie's papers, and he wanted her dead.

Just as he took another pace, he froze still. The intruder heard his ride bucking, loudly neighing its revulsion. Perhaps some scurrying fox or rabbit had startled the horse. It was even possible that the mount had innately sensed the imminent attack, rising up on its hind legs in agitation. The horse's restless whinnies, though, had alerted Lizzie within.

She slammed the door open. The locals in Bethesda had spoken of Lizzie as a reclusive eccentric. They had all described her very fondly: a kind, hard-working old lady. The intruder saw none of that. He only saw a silhouette carrying what was unmistakeably a rifle.

He stiffened, hoping to remain unseen against the blackness. It was futile. A sickly yellow beam shone from the front door, exposing the intruder. In the candle light, Lizzie could see him, but he could not see her.

'You? What the heck do you want?'

Lizzie seemed confused by who she thought she had seen. This slightest hesitation was the only advantage the intruder needed.

He opened fire. Dazzled by the lamplight, the burglar shot blindly. A few random bullets were sufficient, though. Lizzie's silhouette toppled. The prowler skulked over to the corpse. He prodded Lizzie's body with his foot as he reloaded. She only rocked slightly as he nudged her remains with his boot. The lack of response showed that she was dead, but the burglar had plenty more work to do.

As the prowler stepped over Lizzie's sizzling corpse, his horse reared once more. This time, the ride seemed to be desperately fighting to break the reins tying it down. Entering Lizzie's house, the intruder ignored his mount's desperate snorts.

Within, he smiled grimly as he absorbed the welcoming heat. Lizzie's cabin was hospitable and cosy. Even though she had been an old woman, her house was ordered and clean. The downstairs was a single room, which acted as the lounge, kitchen and dining room. A fire cracked pleasantly in the stone hearth. The burglar smelled beef stew on a stove. He took a ladle of it to his cracked lips, and then guzzled a mouthful. An itinerant, the interloper had been on the run almost all of his life. Food and warmth were always distractions. He would have been content to squat for a couple of nights, but there was something he was looking for.

The thief did not know exactly what, reasoning that he would know when he found it. He started with the bureau in the corner. He withdrew the shelf, and then ruffled through the papers within. The burglar discarded them contemptuously. They were not what he wanted. He pushed over furniture and tossed Lizzie's articles on the floor.

He then tried the bedroom upstairs. There were a number of boxes under the bed. The intruder emptied them. They contained keepsakes that were nothing but trash to him. He scattered the contents all over the ground. His ransacking in full passion, he emptied the wardrobes, and threw crockery from the shelves. With childish fever, he was beginning to enjoy his rifling.

Indeed, he grew so absorbed in his sacking that he almost did not hear the voices downstairs. The burglar cursed himself. He should have been faster. His gunshots had drawn somebody to the cabin. He had earlier cased Lizzie's house. There was a back door. The intruder hoped to sprint back downstairs and exit before the visitors could confront him.

He pounded down the steps, where he fired a shot back through Lizzie's downstairs room. There were now three men standing over Lizzie's smoking remains. They looked like farmers, possibly a man and his two sons. The burglar did not care whether he killed or not. He simply wanted to distract them enough to flee. Indeed, they all recoiled fearfully when the intruder's revolver flashed. As they flinched, the burglar retreated hurriedly into the night.

In his haste, the intruder had not concealed the unmistakeable blemish on his cheek. Lizzie's neighbours had seen it clearly before they had jumped back from the housebreaker's bullet. There was only one man in town with such a unique blotch.

The neighbours screamed after the fleeing killer.

'What the heck are you doing here? You are not getting away with this, Abdon Timpson!'

# CHAPTER 2

Abdon had a hundred things to do on Monday morning. Only twenty-one, Abdon was being fast-tracked to the presidency of the Bank of Bethesda. True, Abdon's father was the owner of the bank, but Abdon had never doubted his own gifts.

As junior manager, Abdon was entitled to his own office. Heck, he had insisted on it. Busy as Abdon was, there was time enough for one more peek at the photograph. Abdon withdrew the top drawer of his mahogany desk. The Bank of Bethesda had made a generous donation to the local church and a newspaper had photographed Abdon handing over the cheque. As ever, Abdon was pleased by the sight of the handsome thing in the daguerreotype. He fawned vainly over his own image.

Fabian Timpson, Abdon's father, did not approve of that touch of arrogance. In a futile attempt to teach his son something about humility, Fabian had once told Abdon the legend of Narcissus. Abdon's response had been typically brash.

'A man in love with his own reflection, Dad?' Abdon had grinned. 'What can I say? I plead guilty!'

Lingering over the photograph, Abdon approved of the man he saw. His hair was as black as obsidian. Abdon slicked it with so much oil that, when the grease inevitably dripped, there often appeared to be beads of perspiration on his brow. The banker's moustache was immaculately tweaked by weekly visits to the barber. Abdon would never admit it, but he found his hazel eyes to be rather bulbous and ranine.

Naturally, his most attractive feature was his birthmark. Even in adulthood, it was a bright bloody red. Shaped uncannily like a scythe, there was something unearthly about that blemish.

A humbler man might have felt a little embarrassed by such a striking stain. Not Abdon. When he walked into the saloon, he conceitedly knew that everybody was looking at him. The turned heads as he strutted through Bethesda's bustle gave him a sense of haughty self-satisfaction. Abdon regarded the discolouration as an enhancement, and not a disfigurement. The scarlet crescent moon was also a boon for chatting to the ladies. They listened raptly when Abdon told them that the mark was in fact a tattoo from when he lived amongst the Indians. At other times, it was a scar from a voodoo ritual, or the brand from an encounter with cattle rustlers.

'Quit ogling yourself like a little girl!' Old Man Fifield snapped.

Abdon, rapt as he stared at the newspaper article, had not noticed the senior bank manager entering the office. Fifield made a show of noisily dropping the tellers' ledgers on Abdon's desk.

'Get to work, you darn dandy.'

'Yes sir, Mr Fifield.'

Abdon hurriedly returned the newspaper to the drawer. While Abdon's father owned the bank, Fabian – perhaps in response to Abdon's unhealthy self-regard – had taken measures to ensure that Abdon's banking journey was not an easy one. Fifield, Fabian had made clear, was the boss.

'Mr Fifield has the power to fire you, whether you are my son or not. Do you understand, boy?' Fabian had barked.

Indeed, Fifield had come close to doing just that on a number of occasions. The senior manager, an army veteran, was probably about fifty, but looked like a hundred-year-old. Fifield patrolled the bank, ramrod straight, as a sergeant would rule over the parade square. As overconfident as Abdon was, Fifield's sonorous voice always made him shut up and listen.

Pencil in hand, Abdon began to work his way through the ledgers. Despite his hubris, Abdon did indeed possess a flair and aptitude for banking. Summarizing the ledgers absorbed him, and Abdon soon lost track of time. Fifield had noted his understudy's promise and skill, but was mindful of fattening Abdon's plump ego still further. Abdon, when he was not distracted by dreams of his next bowler hat purchase, could also be very industrious. He took pride in the late nights he put in at the bank. While he always batted away his father's praise with mock disdain, Abdon was in fact touched by Fabian's commendation.

By noon, the ledger report had been finished. At his father's insistence, Abdon's career had started with a lowly cashier's position. He had loathed the silly stripy waistcoat and the petty gripes of unhappy customers, but Abdon had put his brains to work. He had now learned the inner workings of the bank expertly, and was thirsty to learn still more.

Abdon's next chess move would be to do nothing to discourage Fifield's retirement. When the Old Man stepped aside, Abdon would step forward.

'A job well done,' Abdon smirked aloud. 'Even if I do say so myself.'

Grinning smugly, Abdon permitted his mind to wander. He gazed through the bank's window at Bethesda's Monday activity. Small as the town was, it was attracting settlers from all over America. Abdon watched as two cowboys impatiently directed their heads of cattle. The banker secretly found the beasts frightening. They boasted monstrously thick horns. While cows meant cash for Bethesda, Abdon always kept safely away from the steers. The cows answered the coaxing of their human guides with defiant moos. Underfoot, the muddy ground was still hard with frost. It twinkled under the winter sun's sickly glimmer.

Something caught Abdon's eye. Across the street, he spied Caleb Gough. Caleb and his sons, shivering in the cold, were in conference with the sheriff.

Abdon knew Caleb well. A couple of years ago, Caleb had approached him for a small loan. Abdon well-remembered that day. He could tell that Caleb was not at ease stepping into his office. Caleb was a man of granite. The farmer was more comfortable ploughing his fields, or slaughtering his swine with callused fingers, than fidgeting in the alien environment of a bank manager's study. Caleb had not even worn a suit for the appointment. He had, naively, attended wearing muddy boots and filthy dungarees. Caleb had glanced around Abdon's office with nervous, darting eyes.

Of course, Caleb had not resisted a few furtive glances at Abdon's birthmark.

Abdon, though, had an easy charm. He was accomplished at putting prospects at ease. With a courteous handshake and some friendly small-talk, Abdon had persuaded Caleb to drop his guard.

'See, Mr Timpson, I got a big wheat order coming in. Said yes to it before I done thought it through. Going to need a whole new set of tools and such like.' Caleb had inhaled sharply, as if he were steeling himself. 'Need a loan for fifty dollars.'

Abdon knew from Caleb's bank account that the homesteader only eked out a living. On paper, Caleb was not a promising investment. Yet, Abdon had refined an instinct for discerning the good debtors from the bad. Innately, Abdon had sensed that Caleb was a grafter. He had approved the loan.

Six months later, Caleb had returned and repaid the debt early. Abdon had earned the farmer's trust – and a healthy little profit on the gamble.

The Goughs seemed frantic and animated this morning. They gestured across the street at Abdon's window. He waved back. Abdon was accustomed to being pointed and stared at, and thrived on the attention.

The sheriff crossed the strip and entered the bank premises. Intrigued, Abdon left his office to receive the marshal.

'Sheriff, how can I help?' Abdon piped, reaching out to take the lawman's hand. The marshal did not reciprocate.

'Abdon Timpson,' the sheriff commanded. 'You're under arrest for murder.'

# CHAPTER 3

Fifield did not even flinch when Abdon was led away. While inwardly he was perplexed and taken aback, his old soldier's instinct snapped its heels together. On the battlefields, he had seen dear friends butchered. Fifield had never hesitated for an instant, he had been too busy butchering somebody else. Scandalous as the seizure of Abdon was, worse things had failed to tip Fifield's level head.

The queuing customers were gossiping loudly. Not one of them could have possibly known what was happening, yet this did not prevent the gaggle's idle speculation. Fifield overheard snippets of their ignorant opinions. They infuriated him. However, he did not have the time to sit there and seethe. Fifield had to act.

He marched out of the office at pace. Fifield noticed the shoulders of his chief teller tensing as the cashier heard the thumping approach of his manager. This nervous reaction pleased Fifield. His staff ought to be ill at ease around their superior.

'Yes sir?' the teller almost whimpered.

'I'm heading up to see Mr Timpson,' Fifield barked.

'Until I get back, you're in charge.'

The teller was a good man: Fifield had seen to it. He had not been so polished when the manager had first appointed him. However, a few years of Fifield's ear-splitting and exacting instruction had ironed out the man's creases. The teller could be trusted for the rest of the afternoon.

'And I'm borrowing your horse.' The clerk dared not protest.

Without, Fifield was stung by the frigid October air. The bite of the cold seemed to worsen every year. The banker had to squint and grit his teeth as he stiffly mounted the commandeered horse. As the situation was pressing, Fifield attempted to spur the ride with venom. All he could manage, though, was a hard tap. The veteran saw himself as steadfast, rather than patient. His age made commonplace tasks take longer and longer. It aggravated him, but he persevered.

His body ached as it rocked in the saddle. Once a cavalry soldier, Fifield now tried to avoid riding. He told himself that he had a duty to Fabian and his son, that he must contact Fabian immediately. There was far more to Fifield's concern than dutifulness. He had grown to love Abdon as his own son.

Arthritis had caused Fifield's discharge from the army. He had drifted, and chanced upon the Timpson Pawnbrokers in Bethesda. Fifield had had nothing to pawn, but Fabian's office (then but a little kiosk) had had a sign hanging from the desk: 'Help wanted'. Fifield had had barely enough cents for a bowl of grits. The ex-soldier had had nothing to lose.

Shaking hands with Fabian, Fifield's gut had approved.

Fabian had explained his operation. With only a few bucks, Fabian had made loans based on the most pathetic of pawned trinkets. Fabian had been resolute when his borrowers had been unable to buy back their knick-knacks. He had also been scrupulous with his paperwork and had honoured his agreements to the letter. Fabian had often lost money. The defaulted pawns had frequently been worthless garbage that Fabian had been unable to sell. On other deals, though, Fabian had earned a modest profit.

When they first met, Fabian had not been wealthy, yet he had been busy. Fabian had needed manpower, and could just about afford to pay a meagre wage. Fifield had liked who he had seen: his new boss was ambitious and able. Fabian had sensed the same qualities in his new right-hand man.

A pawn shop is a magnet for bums, chancers and scoundrels. Fifield was not a man who suffered fools gladly. His bellow and coarse words had repelled the whingers and wasters. Fabian had been the colonel, writing the battle plan back in his office. Fifield had been the sergeant on the shop floor. The pile of cash in Fabian's safe had accumulated, but the moneyman had been prudent. He had never squandered his wealth. Fabian had been waiting until he had saved enough capital for his enormous gamble: the Bank of Bethesda.

Throughout their business together, Fifield and Fabian had been so busy that their lives had intertwined as intimately as brothers. Fifield had been the best man at Fabian's wedding. The bank's vast profit had permitted Fabian time to start a family. Fifield, however, was too obsessive and serious to wed. To him, the bank was everything. The Timpsons had accepted him as if he were a beloved, if cantankerous, relative.

Indeed, the Timpsons regarded Fifield as the perfect teacher to humble their brash son. Fifield fondly remembered Abdon's first day in school, all the birthdays and Christmases, and even the boy's first words and steps.

That fondness never tempered the tongue-lashings and dressing-downs that Fifield had given young Abdon. During his first months at the bank, Abdon had explored just how far he could irk the Old Man. Abdon had once deliberately left the saferoom unlocked. On another occasion, he had played hooky on a Friday afternoon – just to see if he could get away with it.

Fifield had never surrendered an inch. Even after three years, the veteran had not lost his dedication to roaring in his deputy manager's face. Fifield could see beyond Abdon's shallow self-regard, though. Abdon had inherited his father's intelligence and flair for money-making. Setting aside the bull he talked and the tall stories he invented, Abdon was straight-dealing and honest.

So why had he been detained? Fifield had a feeling he knew why.

The Timpson estate was a couple of miles out of town. Their grand house was an ornate, two-storey building at the rear of a massive garden. That garden was a dirty sea of solid frost under the unforgiving Kansas winter. Fifield had to slow his ride's approach. The crunch of hoofs on the toughened ground could be dangerous. Fifield was not looking forward to this meeting. He inhaled deeply to fortify himself. The steel air only chilled his gorge still further. He coughed, tasting bile. Worry always seemed to make the bitterness in his belly rise.

Dismounting, Fifield was relieved to thrust his hands –

stinging from the gnawing cold – in his pockets. He climbed the stairs to the front porch, and struck the thick oak door with the heavy doorknocker. Its vibrations made his stiffened arm twang uncomfortably.

Fabian answered. He could instantly tell from the look in Fifield's eye that his old friend was distressed.

'Fifield. What is it? Tell me what's up.' Fabian implored.

'Abdon's been arrested. I think it's something to do with . . . well, you know what.'

'This day's been coming for a long, long time, now. I've been dreading it.'

# CHAPTER 4

On Monday evening, Abdon was miserably swallowing lukewarm lumps of porridge in his jail cell. Meanwhile, Gabriel was out on his rounds. The beggar sarcastically referred to his visits as if they were recurring professional appointments. Gabriel did not lie to himself, whoever else he might deceive. He was nothing more than Bethesda's down and out.

The derelict decided to start at José's restaurant. Gabriel was already shivering, but come sunset the cruel cold would tighten its icy fingers still further. The beggar's present abode was a ramshackle cabin just outside of town. The ruin of an old tool-shed, it provided the barest shelter. Whoever owned the collapsing little building, Gabriel thought, must pity him. Either that, or he did not think it was worth the effort of running Gabriel off.

While Gabriel was well-adapted to the chill and the dirt, he was conscious of the mercilessness of the Kansas winter. He had long ago forgotten how old he was, but the tramp was well aware that he was now an old man. Gabriel would benefit from a bowl of soup or a cup of coffee. He needed something warm in his gut a lot more than he needed the spare pennies of some pitying Samaritan.

Bethesda could be colourful and lively during the day, even during October. The day's bustle was now fading, though. As the light died, the town resembled a watercolour painted with pallid greys. There was no jostle to drown out the song of the howling wind.

The frozen mud pressed hard against Gabriel's soles as he trudged shuddering towards José's. The tramp diplomatically knocked on the back door of the restaurant. José answered. He was a burly Mexican who had lived in Bethesda for many years, yet still spoke little English.

'Don't suppose you can spare a few scraps, Señor?' Gabriel asked in the most pitiful tones he could perform.

The down and out pantomimed his request by gawping widely, sticking out his tongue, and pointing at his mouth with a grubby finger. Gabriel had realized that José was not the indulgent type. However, he lacked the language skills to tell Gabriel to get. The Mexican sighed and rolled his eyes. José stepped back inside, then returned with a bowl of hot chilli. He placed it in Gabriel's palms, then made a shooing motion before slamming the door behind him.

Elated by the Latino's impatient generosity, Gabriel returned to the high street with his bowl. There, he sat on the boardwalk, scooping the steaming mince and rice into his maw with his fingers. Such charity was more intoxicating to Gabriel than liquor. The tramp devoured the chilli before sucking his fingers clean with delighted slurps.

José's kindness inspired Gabriel. He felt much more optimistic about his next appointments. While he jokingly called his visits his rounds, Gabriel did maintain a loose routine. The derelict had learned which residents he could approach and the locals who would turn their backs.

Gabriel had created mental notes on his benefactors, and was careful never to hit any individual too often.

Rising to make his way to his next stop, Gabriel caught a glimpse of his reflection in the shop window. It was a comical sight, and the down and out laughed. His tangled beard and wild grey hair were filthy. He wore a stolen great-coat, torn with its lining exposed, that had patently been tailored for a much bigger man.

'How did it come to this?' he joked to himself, setting off.

Perhaps ten years ago, Gabriel had travelled west with nothing but ambition and passion. He had found odd jobs as a farmhand or barkeeper, but had struggled to win the success that other settlers had accomplished. Gabriel still recalled the wretched day when the landlord of the boarding house had finally ejected his most irksome tenant.

What the frontiersmen called manifest destiny, Gabriel had decided, was something that happened to other people. Ranchers and gold prospectors had built empires, but the beggar lacked laces for his leaking boots. Despite his misfortunes, Gabriel remained upbeat and philosophical.

'Any day now, things are going to look up,' was his daily aphorism.

Gabriel's next stop was Alice's house. She was a widow who lived alone. Her husband had been a builder, and he had skilfully constructed a beautiful cottage for them just outside of town. Alice had lost her man to consumption when the couple were still very young. Ever since, Alice had led a spartan, solitary life. She made ends meet by doing laundry, mending and sewing. Despite her bad luck, Gabriel had always found Alice to be gregarious and kind.

Perhaps her experiences had developed in her a sense of empathy. She was always good for a cup of coffee or a sandwich.

Cheered and energized by the chilli, the tramp continued on his stroll to Alice's. While her home was only a short walk from town, Gabriel sought to call in and return to his tumbledown shack before it darkened too much.

Following the dirt path through the fields to Alice's, the derelict paused a moment to wonder at the sunset. Clouds as red as rust clung to the greyed skies, as if the heavens had been powdered by rouge. The grass, rigid with frost, seemed to be clawing free from the soil with icy talons. Beyond, the pale blue of the frost on the plains reminded Gabriel of the colour of lifeless veins. Each wintry breath of wind hissed in his ear with menace. Frissons of cold pulsed through the down and out's sickly flesh. As invigorated as he had been by José's chilli, the coldness and the gloom were beginning to sap Gabriel. He approached Alice's with rapid paces, resolved to complete his house call quickly.

It pleased the beggar to see the lights on, but Gabriel hesitated once again. There was a horse hitched to one of the posts supporting Alice's porch – but Alice did not ride. More than odd, this was eerie. The tramp gulped as icicles seemed to drill through his veins. Alice rarely received visitors, so who was inside?

Gabriel was about to turn back when the figure of a man slammed the cottage door behind him in haste. Fearful, the derelict slipped behind a tree and spied the shadowy intruder as he mounted and rode off into the fields. It was darkening, and Gabriel squinted to make out the fleeing interloper. The beggar could see well in the dark, but he could scarcely comprehend who he had just witnessed.

With that unique birthmark, there was nobody else it could have been.

'Abdon Timpson? The bank manager? What the heck is he doing out at Alice's?' Gabriel wondered. 'And why is he covered in blood?'

# CHAPTER 5

At the sheriff's words, Abdon was unusually speechless. Sheriff Wood was a towering, thickset man whose furrowed face and bellowing voice commanded respect and fear. More than a law enforcer, Wood was a father figure to Bethesda. He would break up fights with a quiet word, but could also overpower crooks and gunslingers with ruthlessness. When Sheriff Wood appeared, he meant business.

He lay a comforting hand on Abdon's shoulder. Unconsciously, Abdon's dumbstruck mouth was agape.

'Come quietly, son. I ain't going to cuff you.'

Mute with shock, Abdon could only nod. Numb and disbelieving, he followed the lawman like an automaton. Wood was practised in playing the role of the lawman. In thirty years of law enforcement, he had gleaned much experience in hiding his emotions. Inwardly, the marshal was profoundly disturbed by Lizzie's murder. As reclusive as she had been, Lizzie had been a good woman. It also bothered him that Abdon was the culprit. As swaggering and cocksure as Abdon was, he had never been in trouble. His customers spoke fondly of him and his influential father. Wood could not fathom the rationale for Abdon's involvement. Criminals, the sheriff had learned, had a certain uneasy aura. This air of lawlessness clung to them like swamp gas. Abdon lacked that crooked ambiance. Yet, the description had been so clear. There was nobody else around with a birthmark like that.

As Abdon was escorted from the bank, the customers all turned to watch. The banker was reminded of a pack of coyotes collectively sniffing the air at the smell of prey. Though Abdon typically thrived on being the centre of attention, the arrest had stunned him.

Abdon, absent-minded, walked awkwardly and stiffly alongside the sheriff. He almost made a couple of wrong turns, and Wood had to take his arm to lead him to the marshal's office. The sudden change in the young banker was unsettling. Abdon had rapidly paled. He seemed to be trying to speak, but could only garble half-formed words. Wood dared not let his pity show in his comportment, but in his breast he felt a touch of sorrow for the boy.

Abdon was all but in a trance when the sheriff walked him into the jail cell. The spartan lock-up was built for two inmates. One of the two simple beds was already occupied by a fat, bald man. He snored contentedly, still wreaking of Sunday night's whiskey.

Wood could see that Abdon was getting nauseous. The lawman put a hand on each of the banker's shoulders, imploring him to sit.

'Take a seat,' Wood directed. As hardened as the marshal was, Abdon thought he detected a touch of concern in Wood's voice. 'You just cooperate, son. I'll get to the bottom of this.'

Abdon nodded meekly. When he heard the jangle of the

turnkey as the steel door clanged shut, Abdon felt dizzyingly unwell. Wood was a little reluctant to be leaving Abdon under the custody of his deputy. The sheriff would have preferred to keep an eye on Abdon. However, there was too much to do. He had to attend to Lizzie's remains, and take formal statements from the Goughs. Wood would also need to examine the scene of the murder, to see what he could learn himself. Most difficult of all, the lawman would need to explain the situation to Fabian Timpson.

The slam of the closing metal door roused Abdon's cellmate. Abdon tensed fearfully as the fat beast stirred. The bald-headed prisoner smiled toothlessly.

'Good morning, stranger.' It was 2pm. 'You're just in time for chow.'

Indeed, Wood's deputy entered shortly afterwards with cups of coffee and chunks of dry bread. The deputy seemed to resent this particular errand, and swiftly exited without a word.

Abdon still felt queasy, but knew that he needed his strength. He forced himself to eat some. His cellmate chattered amiably between noisy slurps of coffee and greedy mouthfuls of bread. Abdon, though, was not listening. Eventually, the cellmate introduced himself.

'By the way, name's Halbert.' There was a moment of hush as Halbert realized who he was bedding own with. 'Say . . . you're the banker guy. The birthmark. Mr Timpson.'

'Yes, partner. Abdon Timpson.'

Abdon battled to conceal the nervousness in his voice.

'Heck, your daddy owns half the county. How come you's locked up with me?'

Halbert himself had been incarcerated for obstinately

refusing to leave the saloon last night. On being frog-marched to jail, Wood had learned that Halbert had a number of outstanding fines. With nobody to bail him out, Halbert would be imprisoned for a number of days. He tended to encounter other petty criminals in jail. Halbert did not anticipate Abdon's candid response.

'I was arrested for murder.'

Another silence. Abdon noticed that Halbert had looked away, and his nonsensical chit-chat had stopped. The bank manager, vain as he normally was, acted for customers from diverse backgrounds. Abdon had advised farmers, cowboys, pensioners, and even millionaires. He was skilled at getting a feel for somebody, and the air in the jail cell had turned chill. It only took a few moments of strained silence for Abdon to discern what was different now.

Halbert was afraid of him. Abdon had been horrified at being imprisoned with a brute such as Halbert. However, the wind vane had now spun.

So edgy were the afternoon and evening that they seemed like days, and not hours. Abdon lay back on the bed, resting his head on his hands. He stared mindlessly at the concrete ceiling. While the sheriff's accusation still seemed incredible, Abdon began to calm.

'Murder?' he thought. 'How could I possibly be caught up in murder?'

It was fantastical. The truth would be exposed. Besides, his father could fix him up with an excellent attorney.

They ate their supper of cold gruel just before sunset. Abdon felt emboldened enough to ask the deputy serving the porridge when he would be released. The deputy curtly told Abdon to wait. Neither Halbert nor Abdon slept for a second that night. Rather, they made cursory, probing glances at each other through the gloom.

When Tuesday's sun-up began to warm the draughty cell, Abdon was exhausted. His dread had made it impossible to enjoy the slightest rest. He felt a prickle of hope when he heard the click of his jailer's keys in the lock.

Wood entered.

'Abdon, come with me,' he ordered.

The sheriff noted that Abdon's eyes were so sunken and blackened that they resembled bruises. Wood also noticed the look of relief on Halbert's face. The lawman closed the cell door after Abdon exited, then fixed Abdon in the eye.

'There was another murder last night. I'm turning you over to your folks. But later on, I'm coming around for a little talk. Somewhere out there, there's a killer that looks just like you. You can't be in two places at once. Can you?'

# CHAPTER 6

Fabian and his wife Ida had arrived to collect Abdon from the jail. They had travelled into town on their private stagecoach after Wood had sent word of their son's release. Fabian stepped down from the stage while Ida waited inside. This struck Wood as odd. The Timpsons, wealthy as they were, had always been friendly and approachable. Wood tipped his hat to Ida within, which she acknowledged with a polite nod.

Fabian seized Wood's hand in a firm handshake. The banker had stern, angular features. His face had wizened and his fair faded to a dirty white. Fabian's piercing blue eyes, though, had never lost their probing gleam. They seemed to flicker and constantly dart left and right, as if he were a wolf scanning his domain.

'Thank you for looking after my son, Sheriff. I am grateful to you for delivering him safe to me.'

Wood had questioned hundreds of liars during his career. Some of them had been masters of deceit, and the sheriff had been hoodwinked. Wood had learned, though. He could spot the giveaways: tiny, almost invisible turns of the head; ums and ahs; or – as in Fabian's case – forced, glib, politeness. The banker had always been an honest man. He had not been born into money. Fabian had always won his customers' trust with the forthright way he had treated them. This morning, though, there was something uneasy about Fabian. The banker seemed to want to get away from the sheriff as rapidly as possible.

'Just doing my job, Mr Timpson.' Wood's poker face betrayed none of his suspicion. 'Abdon,' the sheriff bellowed. 'Come out now.'

Abdon rushed out of the office and embraced his father. It warmed the lawman to see the change in Abdon. The reunion with his parents had transformed him. Abdon was unshaven and unwashed. The clothes he had slept in were crumpled: anathema to an acolyte of fashion such as he. Yet, Abdon was chattering energetically, hugging his father's shoulders with one arm and gesticulating with the other.

Fabian was clearly cheered to see his son. The banker returned Abdon's embraces, but seemed a little embarrassed when Abdon gave Wood a friendly slap on the arm.

'Thanks a bunch, Sheriff,' Abdon chirped with undisguised cockiness. 'You're doing a great job.'

He emphasised his gratitude with a haughty wink.

'Just one thing.' Wood spoke with his customary gravitas. 'I'm going to come and see you both to take statements. It's only routine. Understand?'

Abdon acknowledged his comprehension with an enthusiastic thumbs up. Fabian, though, seemed sheepish.

'Yes, Sheriff. Come and see us any time.'

Fabian's courteous words could not mask his insincerity and reluctance.

*

Wood watched the stagecoach as it trundled away. The vehicle rocked uncomfortably as its wheels milled on the frosty ground.

'What are you hiding?' the lawman wondered.

Within the stage, Abdon, too, was beginning to sense his parents' unease. His long night in the cell had been unsettling. It had been as if a knife had been held to his throat. The feeling of menace had been constant and imminent. To be on his way back home was a great relief. Abdon babbled animatedly about his arrest and incarceration. He only slightly embellished his account of facing down Fat Halbert. The replies and responses of his parents were uncomfortable and monosyllabic. Finally, Abdon had to ask.

'What's up with you two?' he demanded with a touch of indignation. 'Aren't you glad to see me?'

'Son . . .' Fabian paused awkwardly. 'There's something we have to tell you.'

Back at the Timpson house, Fabian led his wife and son indoors. The banker gave the servants some unnecessary errands to get them out of the way. Fabian and Ida were conducting themselves with secrecy and loaded silences. Hardly a patient man, Abdon was growing confused and frustrated.

'Dad . . . Mom . . . what the heck's going on?'

'Follow us up to my study,' Fabian instructed.

Baffled, Abdon complied.

The study was where Fabian carried out his paperwork. It was a large room whose walls were decorated with plush, red wallpaper. The shelves of rare books and luxurious leather settee were very much for show. Fabian had occasionally met his clients here. Indeed, this odd encounter with his parents had the feel of a business meeting.

Fabian and Ida sat behind the desk. They gestured for Abdon to sit in front, almost as if they were interviewing him for a job. Fabian unlocked the little private safe from behind him and withdrew a leather file. He carefully placed the item on a desk in front of him.

'Son . . .' Fabian began.

Ida sobbed. She had in fact seemed to be holding back tears all morning. At first, Abdon had taken this to be her emotion at his return to safety. Now, Abdon did not know what to think. His mother was an ash blonde who kept herself trim tending to the house. She had always proudly done without cleaners and cooks. What had shaken her up?

His father, once again, was hesitating. Abdon prompted him.

'Come on, Dad. Tell me.'

'You know we both love you, Abdon. We love you more than anything in the world. You are our son, but . . . you are not our natural son. Abdon – we adopted you when you were only a new-born baby.'

Abdon said nothing. His father's words were so unbelievable that they had yet to register in his brain. Fabian continued.

The Bank of Bethesda had consumed Fabian's young life. He had ground away tirelessly. By the time he had become wealthy, he was approaching his middle years. Though they had not started a family together, Fabian and Ida had been blissfully happy.

A customer of Fabian had planted an idea in his mind, though. In hindsight, Fabian could see that Calista Richards had been manipulating him from the outset. One day, she had entered the bank to open an account. Soon afterwards, Calista had insinuated herself into the Timpsons' lives. The three had started discussing her private adoption agency.

'That . . . that . . . woman!' Fabian had reddened with rage, his chin trembling.

Ida could sense her husband's anger, and – laying a reassuring hand on his lap – she continued the story.

'We paid Calista the fee for the private adoption. At first, we trusted her. She stuck her claws in us something fierce. Calista was devious, though. Evil. The day you were due to come home for the first time, Calista showed up empty-handed.' Ida wiped away a tear. Her face was flushed with sadness. 'She said there had been a development. Abdon – somewhere out there you have a twin brother.'

# CHAPTER 7

Abdon could have smirked, so unbelievable was his parents' testimony. It was as if they were setting him up for an elaborate, and cruel, practical joke. His mother's tears and his father's angry flush showed that this was no prank, though. Abdon himself could feel his rage swelling in his breast. His fingers whitened as he clenched them in trembling fists. The pulse in Abdon's forehead throbbed and thickened. He wanted to smash that desk to shards and roar in the faces of his parents – if that was what they were.

Somehow, he restrained himself. Freezing as it was outside, Abdon was feverish. Frowning angrily, he undid his collar.

'Go on,' he insisted.

Fabian took up the story.

'Calista told us that another child had been born. Your brother. He was born immediately after you. We could have him, Calista told us, but there was a premium for twins. Well, we were seeing her true colours now. That witch had taken us in. She was so charming. We believed everything she said.

'Now, we were delighted to be taking on two babies. I agreed to pay, but Calista asked for my highest bid.' Still bitter at this sour memory, Fabian rose and began to pace the study.

Unconsciously, Fabian was bending his fingers to make claws. He seemed rapt in this angry recollection.

'My highest bid! It seemed there was another buyer out there. I was so angry, but I named my price and Calista left. The next day, she came back with you in her arms. There was no sign of your twin. That simpering harlot,' he croaked. 'She told us we'd been outbid. And then she got back in her stage and left.'

Fabian returned to his seat behind the desk. He had calmed a little, but his account had drained him. Fabian wheezed uneasily.

Ida carried on.

'Well, we were dumbstruck. I had you crying in my arms, but your father and I just looked at each other like we couldn't believe what had happened. We felt joy and shock and anger and love. And then we got on with it.'

Abdon's composed face was a gentle sea hiding a grasping undertow of rage. Surprised by his own self-control, Abdon picked up the leather file. He unbuttoned it and withdrew the documents within. Abdon flicked through the yellowed papers. His cursory look revealed his name coming up several times. Abdon fixed his so-called father in the eye.

'So what's all this?' Abdon pressed in bold, insistent tones.

Fabian swallowed. He could not meet his son's gaze. Never had his father seemed so meek and ashamed.

'The paperwork,' Fabian confessed. 'Calista had this

funny kink. She ran her darn adoption agency like a business. So she could cover her back with the bank and the IRS. Calista sent out invoices and typed her letters on headed paper. Your . . .' Fabian sighed. 'Your birth certificate is there, too.'

As Abdon rustled through the pages, the ruffle of paper made the hush in the air all the more uneasy. All three wanted to ignore the foul affair, but Abdon's history needed to be faced.

Abdon read Calista's invoice: 'Fee for adoption services.' This home truth was causing the fire in Abdon's gut to blaze and burn with every new detail.

'My birth certificate?' he scoffed. 'It says you two are my parents.'

'That's Calista's doing,' replied Fabian. 'She faked it. At first, she told us it was only a formality, and we believed her. But it was another ruse. Once that birth certificate was in our hands, we were complicit in the fraud. It was a way of keeping us quiet. In case we talked to the law.'

'No law against adoption,' Abdon added coolly.

Fabian rested his head in his hands for a moment, then looked up before responding.

'By chance, I met a midwife at my bank. She told me she'd heard of Calista. Calista had been linked to girls dying in childbirth, babies disappearing and undeclared births. She was nothing but a con woman and a crook . . . and we were dragged into it. And now . . .'

So bizarre had his apparent father's admission been that, for a few minutes, Abdon had forgotten about last night. Sheriff Wood had explained that there was a killer out there with a startling resemblance to him. The obvious connection was not lost on Abdon.

Fabian and Ida jolted when Abdon pounded the desk with his fists. His eyes bulged like a rattlesnake's venom sacs.

'So on top of a lifetime of lies,' Abdon gnashed, 'you're keeping this quiet from the sheriff. Saving your own butts. The reputable banking family.'

'Son . . .' Fabian pleaded, but this single word was the final provocation.

Abdon exploded. He spitefully scrunched his birth paperwork into a ball and stuffed the pages in his pocket. A showman even when rabid, Abdon pounded the study floor. He clambered on to a bookcase and tore down a portrait of Fabian adorning the wall. The weight of the painting made Abdon hunch, but he staggered across the office floor. With a new strength inspired by his fierce wrath, Abdon heaved the painting. The breaking glass seemed to chime musically as the window shattered under the portrait's impact. Fabian felt oddly relieved as the chill without cooled his face. It had grown stifling in his study.

Bawling, Ida ran to Abdon. He pushed her away. As a child, Abdon had been mischievous, but never violent. He had been perpetually hungry to be the centre of attention, yet there had never been any tantrums. Abdon's passionate reaction was unsettling to his mother.

His rampage was not finished. Abdon returned to the desk, and snatched up the silver letter opener. It was an expensive item sharper than a razor. Fabian shuddered as his son brandished the opener like a dagger, his face an ugly mask of intense ire. Abdon turned and stomped over to the sofa. With the opener he stabbed maniacally at the settee, tearing strips from the leather. Abdon screamed inhumanly as his arms worked like pistons.

As unlike Abdon as this frenzy was, some innate knowledge of their son told his parents to wait. Abdon's disfigurement of the couch went on until the smell of leather was rich in the air. Finally, panting and perspiring, Abdon turned to face his mother and father. He said nothing, but merely stood there breathless.

'I still love you, Abdon,' Ida choked through her tears. 'Please forgive us. We'll always be here for you.'

Abdon raised an ostentatious and accusatory finger to his father. His acrid eyes smouldered.

'You two . . . do you know what I'm going to do?'

Fabian gulped. He did not like the sound of this.

'What are you going to do, son?'

With a slow and deliberately affected movement, he withdrew the wrinkled papers from his pocket and untangled the crinkles.

'I'm going to get to the bottom of this. But I've had it with you two liars. Goodbye forever.'

He exited, slamming the door behind him so powerfully that the room shook.

# CHAPTER 8

Almost in a trance, Abdon thundered out of the house. He was both furious and befuddled. The anger in his breast was akin to a piercing pain. His temples pounded, and Abdon could barely think clearly. Images of his parents' confession repeated themselves in his mind.

It was a long walk back into town, but Abdon hardly noticed. He was absorbed in his burning thoughts. His boots made the frozen ground crunch with every pounding footstep. The frigid air might have chilled him were he not so feverishly impassioned.

When he arrived in Bethesda, Abdon was vaguely aware of the heads flickering for a snatched glance. The townsfolk had heard about his arrest, and could not resist gawking. However, they did not know about the secret from the Timpsons' past.

Or did they? Abdon wondered. Everything he knew seemed to be collapsing into dust. His most unshakeable belief had been nothing but an illusion. Abdon could only ponder what other lies he had swallowed.

He headed to the Esplanade Hotel. Abdon reached into his jacket to check his wallet. He withdrew it and checked how much money he had. Keen to instil character in his son, Fabian had never paid Abdon an allowance. Abdon had only earned a deputy manager's salary. Abdon did not quite know what he was going to do next. He hoped he had enough cash. There was no way he was ever returning to that den of deceit.

The Esplanade's manager led him up to his room. There were finer establishments in Bethesda. In other circumstances, Abdon might have lodged somewhere plusher. He would have reasoned that a man of his ability should be accommodated accordingly. Today, though, Abdon was not governed by reason.

The hotelier had worked with the Timpsons before. Abdon was typically so effervescent. The Esplanade's manager could sense his guest's anger, though. Abdon's uncharacteristic surliness hinted at a simmering rage. The hotelier was glad to exit the room and leave Abdon to it.

When the door clicked shut, Abdon sat on the bed. There were tears in the faded grey quilt, and scratches on the wooden furniture. Abdon could hear the muffled sounds of a heated exchange between two guests in another room. There was something faintly dank about the air in his chamber.

Sullenly, Abdon stared at his reflection in the mirror on the dresser. Despite the thin layer of dust, he could discern his own image. Not a day earlier it had been a likeness that Abdon adored. Just as the grime dirtied his reflection, Abdon felt sullied to his core. He wondered if his apparent long-lost brother felt the same. This wicked twin was a killer. Did his brother have any human feelings at all?

'Who are you?' Abdon asked aloud.

He was not certain whether he was rhetorically questioning his brother, or himself.

Abdon had requested a tub of water from the manager. It was lukewarm. Washing himself was unpleasant. The splashes of tepid water on his goose-pimpled flesh made him shiver. With the dregs of the bowl, Abdon wiped the mirror clean. Uncomfortable as his cleansing had been, Abdon felt refreshed. Re-inspecting himself in the mirror, he caught a glimmer of boldness in his eye. Clever, cool, Abdon Timpson – whoever that was – was still in there, somewhere.

'And Abdon Timpson is a cut above,' he reminded himself.

He felt a pang of shame at his destruction of Fabian's study. His father, insufferable as Abdon could be, had always patiently driven and inspired Abdon to excel. That pang was just that, though: merely a pinprick of remorse. Fabian had deceived him since his infancy.

There was an audible groan from Abdon's belly. He had not eaten since that bowl of porridge last night. Formulating vague mental notes of his plan, Abdon headed down to the hotel's bar.

The barroom was quiet on Tuesday afternoon. Abdon ordered a bowl of stew and a jug of water. He wanted to keep a clear head. Abdon read and re-read the crinkled pages from his father's dossier, all the while peeking impatiently toward the kitchen.

When the cheap stew arrived, it was rather a thin broth. The meat had been boiled until it was as tough and grey as rubber. Its carrots and potatoes crumbled under the slightest touch from Abdon's spoon.

It tasted like glue, but Abdon was ravenous. Abdon soon

set his spoon aside and upended the bowl into his hungry maw. So energizing was the broth that Abdon gasped in pleasure having drained the bowl. He was about to order another when he noticed a familiar face entering the bar.

Fat Halbert. His was grinning callously, his eyes fixed on Abdon. As Halbert approached, Abdon sensed something different about him. The half-man, half-hog was ostensibly friendly last night, only raising his guard when he heard of Abdon's alleged crime. Today, he carried an invisible ambiance of belligerence.

Without being invited, Halbert sat opposite Abdon.

'Guess what, Timpson? My brother done paid my fine. Got out just after you. Been celebrating!' he gassed in Abdon's face.

At lunchtime, his cellmate was already in his cups. Halbert rose and came around the table to Abdon.

'So you're no killer after all!' Halbert pressed his palm and stubby fingers on Abdon's cheek and shoved. Irritated as Abdon was, he bit his tongue.

'Is you, daddy's boy?' Another thrust.

In the saloons of Bethesda, Abdon's big mouth and bigger ego had on occasion attracted trouble. He had been challenged to duels and fights, but a black eye or a missing tooth would not do. Abdon had defused these volatile circumstances with his charm. His ability to switch from unbearable vanity to convincing humility was disarming. One moment, an aggressor could be seizing Abdon's lapels. Five minutes later, the same man would be buying Abdon a drink.

Halbert's spiteful pushes would not be neutralized by persuasion, though. Abdon decided not to talk his way out of this fight. Halbert was accustomed to those he bullied acquiescing to him. He always preyed on those smaller, or weaker, than himself.

The sting of Abdon's fist knocked Halbert on to his back. Stunned by the blow, it took him a few seconds to realize what had happened.

Abdon, too, was surprised by his own physical strength and vicious resolution.

'What was that all about, Abdon?' he asked himself as he returned to his bedchamber. 'Who are you?'

# CHAPTER 9

The manager rapped on the door of Abdon's room early on Wednesday morning. Abdon sprang out of bed and collected the bowl of lukewarm water that the hotelier was delivering. He had been awake for a while, anyway. Abdon's blow to Halbert's fat face had tired him more than he expected. True, Abdon had struck with only a solitary punch before Halbert had crawled away like a crab. Abdon was no brawler, though. Throwing but one punch had made him breathless.

'But what a punch!' he had smiled to himself. Despite his confrontation with his parents, that spark of vanity in him continued to glow.

Early that day, Abdon's bruised knuckles had started to throb. The pulsing ache had awoken him. He had lain in the darkness, opening and closing his fingers as he had watched the crystal white winter dawn later through the holes in the mouldy curtains. Outside, Bethesda was stirring. Tradesmen were grumpily calling to each other. Steers ululated reluctantly as cowboys pressed the animals onwards. Abdon shivered, but steeled himself to wash in the cool water. At home, Abdon was accustomed to a hot bath every night and a fresh, pressed shirt every morning. He would not be indulging in such luxuries for a while. Abdon had no firm plans whatsoever for what he was going to do next. He was not going back to his parents, nor was he going to show up at the bank.

The thought of the bank aroused another twinge of shame. Old Man Fifield had been much more than a boss. He had been akin to an uncle, or even a second father. As exacting and ill-tempered as Fifield was, it had pleasured Abdon to show off to him. Fifield had once given Abdon two hours to cash up for the day. Abdon had not attempted to conceal his smugness when he had done it, flawlessly to the last penny, in twenty minutes. What would Fifield think when Abdon did not show up for work?

Abdon stopped thinking about it. Fifield and Fabian were like blood brothers. Abdon imagined that Fifield had been party to the secret as well.

There was only one thing that Abdon wanted to do: find this Calista character. His unwashed shirt and suit felt like a pit of snails had been crawling around their insides, leaving their slimy trails. Abdon attempted to ignore the grubby sensation as he pounded the stairs back down to the bar. He needed a cup of coffee. Strong.

The aroma of the coffee brewing revived Abdon. He could discern between the smells of the finer and the cheaper beans. The Esplanade was not serving the better variety this morning. When the pot arrived at Abdon's table, though, he hurriedly poured a cup, which he gulped. The thick, black, ooze burned his throat, but Abdon could almost immediately feel the treacle restoring him.

He poured another cup, which he sipped more

leisurely. Abdon re-read the so-called birth documents for perhaps the hundredth time. The invoice from Richards Midwifery and Adoption Services had been typewritten. It was headed by the business name and business address. The location of this enterprise was in White Rock: only a couple of hours on the train from Bethesda. It had been more than twenty years since his 'birth', but – at least according to his father – this Calista woman had been well known in her field. There was a possibility that she was still around. If not, perhaps there was somebody that remembered her.

The notion that this was a matter best left to the law flickered through Abdon's mind, but he arrogantly brushed the idea away. Abdon wanted to know the full truth, and he lacked the patience to twiddle his thumbs while Sheriff Wood bumbled towards the answers. It was needless to say that Abdon, at least in his own view, was possibly a little smarter than the sheriff.

Abdon reached for the coffee pot and poured it, only to find the vessel empty. He had been so absorbed in his thoughts that he had unconsciously drained the whole jug. While Abdon could have done with another coffee, it was time to press on.

Outside, Bethesda was busy. Abdon zigzagged through the cows sluggishly walking the high street. Their gentle moos signalled that the steers would only move at their pace, and nobody else's. The pure, chilled air made the whiff of manure all the more noticeable. Abdon shrugged his trembling shoulders to try and keep warm, exhaling a creamy mist as his boots hit the hard ground.

He made his way toward the railway station. At his father's knee, Abdon had been told that Bethesda had once been but a handful of homesteads. The Topeka-Dodge line had transformed Bethesda. Still a comparatively small settlement, the town was growing. His fingers tingling from the incessant coldness, Abdon gave his wallet another quick inspection. He had a few dollars – enough for the ride to White Rock. Though Abdon did not anticipate ever returning to the bank, he had not thought about how he would earn money to feed and clothe himself. Abdon was not happy-go-lucky. Rather, his innate self-belief told him that his superior abilities would handle just about any challenge that could be thrown at him.

Pacing the boardwalk to the station, Abdon glanced across the street. He thought he saw a familiar face, and double-taked. Abdon could only see the face in flickers through the march of cattle. The mug was also misshapen by a bruised eye as thick and black as a rotten banana. When Abdon realized that it was Halbert, he could not resist taking a third look.

'Did I really do that?' he asked himself.

That blackened eye was the result of Abdon's defence. The ugly sight gladdened him, and his last few steps to the station had a bounce to them.

On the platform, the train had already arrived. Abdon had travelled on the locomotive a few times and they had always seemed like iron monsters to him. The hiss of steam and the thunder of the spinning wheels were akin to a dragon taking flight. Today, though, Abdon felt no such childish excitement as he bought his ticket and boarded. He took a seat and stared pensively out of the window. Abdon could only guess what awaited him in White Rock. He tried to imagine what sort of woman bought and sold babies.

Sheriff Wood, on spotting Abdon on the high street, had followed him discreetly. The lawman's curiosity had been pricked.

'Where are you going?' Wood wondered as he spied Abdon getting on the locomotive. 'What are you up to?'

# CHAPTER 10

Wood had no idea what could be on Abdon's mind. The sheriff's instinct, though, told him that the young banker was meddling. Abdon ought to be back with Fabian. A night with Halbert could be unsettling, even for hardened deadbeats. Instead of convalescing or resting, though, Abdon was striking out to who knows where. As experienced as Wood was, you did not need to be Dupin to surmise what was happening. There was nothing odd about a little dirt on one's boots in a muddy cattle market like Bethesda. Abdon, though, was typically faultlessly attired. This morning, he was wearing the same creased garments that had adorned him during his incarceration.

Wood had not liked Fabian's uneasiness when he had arrived to collect his son.

Now, Abdon was leaving town. There had been a bust-up at the Timpson home, and Abdon was taking matters into his own hands. The sheriff had always indulged Abdon's arrogance. Despite his vanity, Abdon was an honest man. His father's bank had done much to help Bethesda prosper. This morning was something different, though. Abdon was naively wading into deep, perilous waters.

The sheriff wanted to sigh. He would need to interrogate the Timpsons and hopefully catch up with Fabian. Right now, though, he had police business.

The steam train piped its horn so sharply that Wood winced as the locomotive departed. In the crisp air, the warmth emanated by the mighty engine was welcome. The pistons worked the wheels, and with the smell of burning coal heavy in the air the train seemed to crawl forward. In moments, it was gone.

Wood wanted to investigate the Adams residence. He had given the crime scene a brief examination on Monday. Alice's death and the arrest of Abdon had delayed this, though. It was presently time to give Lizzie's cabin a proper look in daylight.

Wood's horse was hitched to the rail outside his office. Mounting up, he felt rigid and stiff in the biting air. His ride, though clad in a horse blanket, also seemed uncomfortable in the stinging cold. The mount was restless, signalling its impatience with agitated neighs and thick bursts of steam from its nostrils. Wood, too, was keen to set off. He hoped that the motion of rocking on the saddle would warm his bones.

Riding across the fields to Lizzie's, Wood had to shield his eyes from the blinding glare of the white winter sun reflected in the frost. The lawman rode at a steady pace, anxious to reach the house, but mindful of protecting his mount's hoofs. The horse's feet beat out a regular drum. Wood swayed awkwardly in the saddle as the reverberations of the hoofs on the hard ground shook him. The lawman grasped the horn so tightly that his fingers began to sweat.

Arriving at Lizzie's, Wood remarked how pretty the homestead appeared in the daylight. This illusion was quickly dispelled when Wood entered the little house. Lizzie had been murdered. Her house was eerily silent. Remote from the other homesteads, Wood could not even hear the ululations of cows. Worse than the physical signs of the struggle, though, was the aura that the cabin emanated. It was not so much a sense of menace. Rather, it was a filthy sensation. Something pure and goodly had been despoiled in this house. Wood shivered, but not from the cold.

The sheriff looked around, painstakingly stepping over the debris of broken furniture and shattered possessions. Wood began to imagine what Lizzie's day-to-day life must have been like.

Bethesda's people were paradoxically both close-knit and extremely private. Last year, a house had caught fire. On seeing the angry orange column rising up to the sky through a black mist, almost everybody in Bethesda had stopped what they were doing to fight the blaze. With almost mystic coordination, the townsfolk had formed a human chain. Buckets of water had been manually handed from link to link until the inferno had been quelled. The house had been mercifully empty, but the family that owned it had lost everything. However, the community had kindly taken the family into their own homes. Over the following weeks, the men of Bethesda had taken time out of their punishing routines to rebuild the scorched house.

Yet, in a territory as vast as Kansas, a single homestead could embrace acres and acres. Neighbours might not recognize each other when they crossed on the street. The locals valued their privacy and independence. Families such as the Goughs would bravely protect the vulnerable, but would without hesitation slam their door in the faces of busybodies or snoopers. Indeed, in Bethesda, trespass was tantamount to suicide.

Lizzie herself had been extremely private. She seemed to have been around forever, yet nobody knew much of her background. Lizzie had probably boasted coal black hair once, but her mane had been discoloured by chalky streaks. It was difficult to place her age. She could have been as young as forty, or even much older. While the sun had leathered her face, she had been lean and strong. Lizzie alone had tended her fields and collected her grain. Her routine must have been backbreaking. Lizzie had been a character who, though little was known about her, seemed to know everybody. She had always had five minutes to chat during her occasional visits into town. Her chatter had never been more than small talk, though. Never had she revealed anything personal or intimate.

Studying her home, despite the debris, Wood sensed that Lizzie had been house-proud. There were hooks on the walls for pots and pans. The shelves, while they had been emptied of crockery, were spotless.

Wood spied a keyring on the floor, and plucked it from the mess. The lawman wondered if the key would unlock Lizzie's safe. The lockbox had been concealed in a wooden cabinet, which had now been smashed. Wood tried a key. The lock was reluctant to comply. Rust had stiffened the orifice, but with a few stiff twists of his wrist the sheriff unlocked the safe. It obviously had not been opened for a long time.

There were yellowed pages inside the box. Wood took them out and leafed through them. The papers felt dry and dusty under his fingers, and their must tickled his nose. Studying the fragile documents, the lawman was careful not to tear nor rip them.

The sheriff could speak a touch of Spanish, and – despite his schoolmaster's scolding – a touch less of Latin. Though Lizzie's secret papers were not in English, the lawman could guess what certain phrases signified.

'Elbieta Adamski' sounded similar to Lizzie Adams. 'Polski' meant Polish.

# CHAPTER 11

Abdon sat in the passenger carriage. Thankfully, he was the only traveller that day. Abdon was in no mood for chitchat; he only wanted to brood and stare out at the frozen fields. The passenger cabin was a little dank and gloomy. Abdon rested his head back on the maroon felt seat. The carriage rocked gently as the steam engine powered away. As satisfying as the scent of burning coal was, Abdon was not enjoying the journey.

His mind returned to his hunt for Calista. Again, Abdon wondered what kind of woman she was. His father had nearly been foaming at the mouth when he had described her. It would take a particularly calculating woman to manipulate a man as shrewd as Fabian. She would also be, Abdon imagined, cold-hearted to the point that glacial meltwater ran through her veins. To broker young children for profit, and pretend that you were providing a valued service, took a special kind of callousness.

Thoughts of Calista led to thoughts of Abdon's brother. Fabian and Ida had raised Abdon as an only child. To learn that he might have a sibling – and a twin at that – was a shock. Abdon felt no longing nor love for this errant brother. Indeed, he did sound like a remorseless killer. Abdon was intrigued, though. What was his twin like? Why had his brother suddenly ridden in to Bethesda?

When Abdon had trashed his father's study, then nearly broken his fingers on Halbert's face, his behaviour had been uncharacteristic. He had always been so mindful of avoiding conflict. There was a niggle in Abdon's mind that, no matter how strongly he tried to ignore it, would not relent. Was he similar in any way to this mysterious twin?

Though his mind was in turmoil, Abdon made himself close his eyes. The motion of the locomotive soon swayed him into sleep. Had he known who was watching, Abdon would not have dropped his guard.

Halbert had noticed Abdon eyeing him back on Bethesda high street. The sight of that slick moneyman had caused bitter frissons of anger in Halbert's jowls. He was not accustomed to being bested in any physical confrontation, least of all by a snooty pen-pusher. When he was out of Abdon's sight, he had crossed the road and stealthily followed him back to the train station. Halbert, an experienced cutthroat and mugger, was skilled at disappearing into the crowd.

Halbert's brother had a half-decent job as a ranch hand. He had promised to meet him on Wednesday morning. His brother had offered to fix Halbert up with some work and he had agreed. His brother had bailed him out on countless occasions, and it was high time Halbert started repaying him.

Halbert's perfunctory good intentions were immediately dispelled when he watched Abdon climbing on to the train. Instinctively, he had slipped into one of the cattle trucks. Neither the farmyard stink nor the danger of riding shoulder to shoulder with the cows had deterred Halbert. He had often recklessly stowed away in the same carriages as animals.

Halbert had jolted when the train had animated. He had squeezed through the warm bodies of the beasts as they had ululated their indignation. Halbert was determined to snake through the locomotive's carriages until he reached his prey: Abdon. From cabin to cabin, Halbert fought through the throngs of cows. He heedlessly leapt across the spaces between the carriages, though the slightest slip would have dropped Halbert into a pulverising demise on the tracks.

Halbert was not guided by reason, but by a bitter longing to avenge himself. It was this bloody-mindedness that had motivated his carousel ride back and forth between jail and the streets. The merest slight would fuel a poisonous rage in Halbert. Though he could not read, Halbert maintained a long mental list of those who had wronged him. Right now, that uppity banking brat was at the top of that list.

He reached the platform at the rear of the passenger cabin. The thundering swish of the locomotive masked the padded sound of his feet landing on the metal surface. Halbert peered through the window of the carriage. Abdon was alone.

'Good,' Halbert thought.

Resolved as he was to settle the score, Halbert was conscious that daddy's boy had already beaten him once.

'Won't make that mistake again,' he muttered, withdrawing his Colt from its holster. While vengeful, Halbert was at core a coward. He would have happily shot Abdon in the back of the head. However, Halbert wanted that stuck up toff to see who was standing over him when Halbert pulled the trigger.

With careful steps, he approached Abdon. The rocking train made his paces a little uneasy, and he grasped at the seats for balance.

He found Abdon snoozing in his seat.

'Hey! Bank man! Wake up!' he snarled, wild-eyed.

Instantly, Abdon was alert. When he saw the revolver pointed at him, Abdon did not panic. Indeed, the peril so nigh made him view the predicament with ruthless clarity. Rattlesnake rapid, he seized Halbert's wrist and wrenched it anticlockwise. Halbert's fat fingers and sloppy reflexes were too sluggish activate the trigger. There was a sickening click as his wrist snapped.

Abdon's heart pulsed as the Colt thudded on the carriage's dusty wooden floor. His assailant had been too lazy or complacent to cock the weapon, and the six-shooter did not fire. As Halbert fell to his knees cradling his forearm, Abdon felt nothing but scorn. Calmly, Abdon stood to retrieve the Peacemaker.

Just as it had in the jail cell, the power had seesawed. Abdon trained the .45 on Halbert. He pathetically shielded his face. The fat hog's bawling was beginning to irk Abdon.

'Sit!' Abdon commanded, pointing at a seat. Halbert meekly complied.

'What are you playing at, Halbert?'

Unaccustomed to firearms, the Colt felt heavy and awkward in Abdon's clammy fist. It pleasured him to watch Halbert cower as Abdon thumbed back the hammer with a satisfying clack.

'You could finish off this wretch and the law would be on your side,' Abdon thought, but stopped himself.

'Tell you what, Halbert. I'll let you off at the next stop. I can do without the likes of you. Give me your gun-belt.'

Halbert obeyed dejectedly. Abdon noted that the leather band stored plenty of ammunition. He had a feeling that he would need it.

# CHAPTER 12

'Come in, Abdon,' Calista simpered as she opened her heavy oak door to her guest.

She had spotted Abdon's approach through her window. Calista had had to squint through her spectacles to identify the visitor. With that birthmark, though, she had a pretty good idea who her caller was.

Abdon was taken aback for an instant, but quickly remembered why he was here. He stormed into Calista's house as she affectedly turned away from him. Calista sat back in a rocking chair. In a deliberately provocative silence, she lit an expensive cigar that was almost as thick as a cucumber.

She lived in a costly brick house just outside of White Rock. Abdon had found Calista very easy to locate. Her address matched the one on her invoice. When Abdon had asked for directions, White Rock's locals had been brusque and terse. They all knew the address, but did not seem to want to chat about it. The house must have cost Calista a few bucks. It made Abdon wonder just how prolific her adoption racket was.

Within, the house did not resemble a private home.

Though the furniture was luxurious, Calista's front room was more like an archive. It reminded Abdon of the filing room in his bank. The shelves and shelves of dossiers were neatly and diligently organized. While the room was fastidiously tidy, it wreaked of stale cigar smoke.

'How can I help you, Abdon?' Her tone was heavy with sarcasm. Calista could expertly enchant a new prospect, but she had no need to charm a Timpson. She had already taken their money.

Abdon paused for a moment, simmering as he studied Calista. She may well have been stunningly beautiful at one time. Her hair dye still made her curls look a fiery red. Fine lotions had preserved her flesh's creamy colour. Too many cigars had begrimed her teeth, though. Her contrived smiles were as black as rotten scars.

He stood over her, pulling the birth papers from his pocket and making a show of displaying them. Calista laughed hollowly.

'Haven't seen them for a while, Abdon.'

'Tell me.'

'Tell you what?' Calista drew cruel delight from toying with the young man.

Abdon exploded. He pounded a table with his fist, the impact making the whole room shake.

'Tell me what happened, darn it!' he roared.

The air in the room was volatile, but Calista was unmoved. She had dealt with angry customers before. They did not frighten her in the slightest. Calista sucked theatrically on her smoke, the cigar end winking devilishly.

'Some twenty years ago, two women came to see me. Sisters. They were Polish settlers – real clannish like. The daughter of one was in the family way. She was very, very young. Too young to marry. Well, that's where I make my money. I didn't charge the Adamskis. They were broke, anyhow. Told them I'd place the little baby with . . .' Calista could not resist giggling. 'With a loving family.'

Abdon felt nauseous. He sat down, his head dizzied. It was not comfortable to face up to Calista's truths.

'I already had Fabian Timpson set up. He paid me a pretty penny. But it was a baby bonanza! After you, darling little Zofia popped out your kid brother. Or maybe it was the other way around.'

'The other way around?' Abdon spat.

'You both had those crazy birthmarks, you dumb ass. And I didn't care which was which. Now Daddy Timpson didn't want to pay for two babies, but I've always got buyers queuing up.'

Caustically pantomiming a dutiful secretary, she melodramatically inspected her files.

'Ah,' she gasped, pulling a dossier out. 'The Lehane file.' Calista handed a yellowed sheet of paper to Abdon, which he snatched. 'You take that, Abdon. It's the address of your brother's family.' She patted Abdon on the shoulder, and he had to fight not to recoil from her sickening touch. 'All part of the service, partner.'

'What's all this paperwork bull?' Abdon demanded. 'You sell babies. Not real estate.'

Calista returned lethargically to her rocking chair.

'Everyone in White Rock knows what I do. They don't like it, but they still take my money. My mortgage is settled and my servants are well paid. I'm the best customer at the tailor and the drugstore. If I show a piece of paper typed up all neat and pretty, it makes me look legit. And you can remind your mom and dad about that fake birth certificate they've been passing off as real.'

'That was just a trick to keep them quiet.'

Calista puffed as she pretended to look philosophically up at the ceiling.

'That what they said to you? Funny that we call them "half-truths". Why not "half-lies"? They paid me to fake it so they could pass you off as their natural child. Your parents knew exactly who I was and what I did. They're up to their necks in it. And they don't want anybody snooping into . . . well, you know what.'

She winked ironically.

'No. I do not know what.'

'Young Zofia. She did not survive childbirth. Her family didn't want a fuss, so I kept the whole thing quiet. But Daddy Timpson knew about Zofia. And he couldn't have his good name dirtied like that.'

Abdon trembled with rage. He longed to take this evil witch's neck in his hands and make her choke. It was uncanny to think that the young girl Calista described had been Abdon's natural mother. He did not doubt the unsettling reality of Calista's heartless words. However, the distressing truth did not change Abdon's feelings. This Zofia girl was nothing but a stranger to him.

This brother, though, intrigued him. Abdon had been raised an only child. While he had been a popular boy on the schoolyard – even in childhood Abdon's self-regard had been strong – he had sometimes wished for a companion who shared his brains and ability. It seemed, though, that his deadly double was nothing more than a cutthroat.

'What happened to my twin?' Abdon implored. He hoped that his desperation could not be heard in his voice.

'Like I said. I sold him to the Lehanes. Never heard anything since. Go and check them out. They only live a train ride away. When you meet the Lehanes, though, you'll be mighty glad you didn't end up with them.'

# CHAPTER 13

Abdon had to restrain himself as Calista rose to see him to her door. The air of evil she radiated was almost palpable. Calista could sense his disgust, and it gladdened her. Her customers often looked at her with scornful eyes, before begrudgingly paying her fee. It thrilled her to know that she could rile somebody so.

'Nice to meet you properly, Abdon. Safe journey now.'

Though Abdon was angrily biting his tongue, Calista could not resist slapping him on the back as he departed. Her gesture made Abdon shudder before he stamped away without another word. Abdon peered back over his shoulder, though, with fury in his eyes.

Calista returned to her rocking chair, and her cigar. She was as busy as ever. Desperate men and women wrote to her or knocked on her door with regularity. At first, she always embraced them with warmth and a sympathetic ear. With youngsters, she often implored them to call her Aunty Calista. Her hugs and sweet words were all part of the act.

While her trade was much in demand, Calista enjoyed

the great deal of leisure that her business permitted. She had to meet the families involved, go to pains to keep them separated, and attend to the births themselves. Each deal only took a few days, though. There was ample time for relaxing in her chair with a smoke, or a shopping trip, or a few lazy hours in the teahouse. Calista was a solitary person. Her business needed secrecy, and Calista had little time for anybody that could not make her money.

For appearances, she would occasionally get stuck making small-talk with White Rock's locals. Without asking directly, Calista would chatter about the price of things and how hard she was working. She was only ever curious about one thing: how much do you earn? With the snatches of information gleaned, Calista would try to guess how much money the other person made. Inevitably, Calista was making more. She felt scorn for anyone that could not match her earning power.

Calista's first deal was a fond memory for her. Even years and years later, she still marvelled at her masterstroke. Calista and her mother had been charladies. They had lived in an impoverished shack just outside White Rock. It had never been entirely clear to Calista what had happened to her father. Her mother had spoken fleetingly of him as a 'worthless bum' and a 'no-good varmint'. She had been a bitter woman as full of rage as a boil is bloated with pus. She had been a rigid disciplinarian to Calista, scolding and punishing her for the slightest mistake. While their hovel had been leaky and freezing cold, its interior had been meticulously clean. Calista had been expected to scour the pots and pans to spotlessness with water she collected from the river. The rags they wore, while torn, were always scrubbed clean.

While her mother had been strict, she had also been fiercely protective. She worked what seemed like endless hours to provide for her daughter. As poor as they were, Calista had gone to the schoolhouse. Even though she had toiled to provide the best for her daughter, it was not long before Calista joined her mother on her cleaning rounds.

Between them, they had held down several jobs. One of Calista's positions had been as a servant girl in a mansion house. There, as Calista had mopped or swept or wiped, the lady of the manor would talk relentlessly about her selfish problems. Her husband had frequently been away on business trips, and her children had been away at boarding school. Ma'am had often been lonesome, and Calista had grown into her only confidante. She would nod and smile and gush, while inwardly loathing her layabout mistress and her imagined tribulations. The woman of the house had alluded to her extramarital romances, and one day madam had tearfully broken down in Calista's arms. She was with child.

'Whatever can I do, Calista?'

Every night, Calista's mother had discussed her work. It was as if she was setting an example for her child on how she should be working. Lately, Calista's mother had been cleaning for a wealthy couple who had been childless. How they had self-pityingly whined and whinged of their plight! When Calista learned of ma'am's predicament, she had felt as if a jigsaw piece in her mind had been put in place.

'Ma'am – I might be able to help!'

Calista had acted as a messenger between madam and her husband. The lady of the house was ill and would be going away to convalesce. Her husband had scarcely noticed. Meanwhile, Calista's mother – impressed by her daughter's ingenuity – had approached her own employers with a suggestion.

The birth of madam's lovechild had been an unsettling experience for Calista. Though she advertised herself as a midwife, she had learned everything on the job. She had been improvising, with a forced calm demeanour. Calista had been relieved when the child had finally arrived and she could deliver the stock to its new owner.

The money that the deal had created had enabled a rare period of luxury for Calista and her mother. They had shopped together, and enjoyed thick steaks at the café. The two had laughed and chattered, pleased by their inventiveness and good fortune. As callous as Calista had grown, she remained proud that her ploy had allowed a comfortable ending for her mother. Her punishing life had prematurely transformed her into an old woman. Shortly after the baby trade, her mother had slipped away. Calista had used the last of the money to pay for the funeral.

Calista had returned to the mansion house. With the secret she was hiding, her employment there had been secured. Calista had imagined that the sale she had set up had been purely fortuitous: a lucky one-off. While she had gone back to indulging ma'am's gripes and complaints, her mistress had taken Calista aside for a quiet word.

'Calista – I have another favour to ask. You see, I have this friend . . .'

Calista supposed that she was still a cleaning lady, only now a much more expensive one. Dirt did not always mean dust, or grime. The sordid affairs of the rich were dirty in a different way.

She swayed her rocking chair, drawing deeply on her cigar. Calista wondered what Abdon would think of the Lehanes.

# CHAPTER 14

Marching back into town, Abdon was furious. Calista was a monster. She traded babies for cash and laughed behind the backs of the hopeless people she exploited. Calista had presided over the death of Zofia. She looked back at the episode matter-of-factly, as if a steer in a cattle drive had drowned fording a river. His mind thrashing, Abdon was finding it hard to square the facts. While he was angry at Calista's neglect of Zofia, Abdon found it difficult to accept that Zofia had been his natural mother. Could he truly be the illegitimate son of a Polish settler? The whole idea of it seemed fanciful – but it was true.

Abdon tried to focus his mind on his next steps. He read the invoice Calista had given him. It was addressed to a house in Cowbridge – the next stop on the railroad. It was starting to get late. The shadowy horizon was rising to hide the fading sun. Abdon hardly noticed the temperature plummet yet further. The angry energy in his pounding strides warmed him. As he neared White Rock, the town's bustle was waning into a hush interrupted by the odd roar of laughter from the saloon.

Approaching town, Abdon checked his wallet once

again. His funds were running low. It looked like he would be spending another night in a hotel. There was some money in his personal account back at the bank, but that was the last place Abdon wanted to go. He had set off on his private enquiries on a sudden impulse. Abdon had not made any plans for when his money ran out.

White Rock seemed grey and wintry in the evening gloom. Abdon followed the sound of merriment from the saloon. He was relieved to see a vacancy sign on the saloon's door. As low as Abdon was getting on cash, he did not relish the idea of shivering on a train station platform all night.

Entering the bar, Abdon could sense all eyes on him. The saloon was busy. Through a mist of blue smoke, Abdon noticed card players and drinkers sneaking glances. They were no doubt wondering about this odd stranger with such a distinctive birthmark. As comfortable as the glow from the fireplace was, Abdon was glad when the barkeeper led him up to his room.

Abdon could only afford a bowl of soup, which he asked to take in his bedchamber. He lit the dusty oil lamp, but it did little to brighten the dingy room. He could still hear the muffled laughter and song from the saloon below. The dank little bedchamber had a chill, and Abdon savoured the warmth from the soup bowl as he raised it directly to his chapped lips.

As angry as he had been at Calista's, his rage had cooled. Despite himself, the mustiness and cold in the hotel room made him long for home. Though it had only been two nights, Bethesda now felt as if it was a thousand miles away. He undressed and, though it was still early, got into bed. The slight sheets felt icy at first, but after pulling them over his head, the bed soon warmed.

He fought to keep thoughts of his mother and father out of his head. His mind meandered nonetheless.

Fabian Timpson was a military aficionado. He had never worn the uniform himself, but he loved to hear Fifield's army anecdotes. Fabian was also a collector. During his pawnshop days, he would set aside collectibles such as medals or regimental flags for his private perusal. When he started making big money at the bank, Fabian would treat himself to rare antiques. He had even splashed out on a suit of armour imported from Europe. Fabian's favourite piece, though, was a British rifle from the American Revolutionary War. He had nicknamed it the Limey.

Fabian kept the Limey under lock and key in a heavy oak cabinet in his lobby. As a child, Abdon had been fascinated by the weapon. It was over a hundred years old, or so his father said. Mr Fifield (and even in boyhood, Abdon had to call him Mr Fifield) had – at least in the story – plucked the rifle from the stiff fingers of a slain Englishman. Fifield was a lot younger than a hundred, but this was a deduction that Abdon had not yet made. He would pester his father and Mr Fifield with endless questions about the rifle. Finally, Abdon had squeaked with delight when Fifield had offered to show him how it worked.

Fifield, Abdon and his father had strolled out to the woods behind the house. This had to be in secret, Fifield had insisted, in case the British were spying on him. So enthralled had Abdon been that he had bounded energetically as they had approached the woods.

Fabian had taken meticulous care of the Limey. It was

still functioning, and Fifield was a skilled rifleman. Abdon had watched, his mouth agape, as Fifield has sprinkled black powder into the chamber, pulled back the lever, and squeezed the trigger. Fifield had been mindful of firing into the air. The thunder from the old weapon had caused Abdon's ears to ring. The smell of the gunpowder had reminded Abdon of ground coal.

'Would you like to try, Abdon?' Fifield had asked with his customary seriousness.

'Sir, yes sir!' Abdon had piped in wonderment.

Abdon had then been so little that Fifield had had to kneel down beside him. Fifield had loaded another round, then guided Abdon's tiny fingers along the weapon.

'Watch out now, young man. This weapon will recoil. It might hurt your shoulder some.'

'Don't worry, sir.' Even in childhood, Abdon had possessed a seed of cocksureness.

Pulling that trigger and making the Limey explode had thrilled Abdon to his core. The kickback from the weapon had indeed been hard. The next day, though, Abdon had been showing off the bruise on his shoulder to his friends. During the walk back to the house, Abdon had talked nonstop of his experience with the rifle. His father and even Mr Fifield had been grinning.

Snuggling in the pleasing warmth beneath the bedsheets, Abdon sniffled. Revisiting that treasured memory had caused him to shed a tear. Once more, his destructive tantrum in his father's office haunted him. Inwardly, he tried to convince himself that his childhood memories were lies. His words felt hollow, though. Fabian and Ida had raised him as their own kin. They had sheltered him, fed him and clothed him. Yet, here he was in White Rock, sulking in a filthy hotel room. It was difficult for Abdon, vain as he was, to admit it to himself. He was already missing his parents.

Abdon brushed those soppy thoughts out of his mind. Tomorrow, he would find the Lehanes and learn a little more about his weird doppelgänger.

# CHAPTER 15

'Balam? Is that you? I thought you were in jail!'

Janet Lehane stepped forward to embrace Abdon, but he pushed her gently away. She was a pretty young woman, Abdon noticed, a little older than himself. Despite her shining blonde hair and rosy skin, her beauty was tainted by an ugly black eye and a missing tooth.

The train had pulled in to Cowbridge earlier that Thursday morning. In Cowbridge, it seemed, everybody knew the Lehanes.

'What do you want those crazies for, partner?'

'They're right down the road, but keep away from that madhouse.'

They lived in a well-appointed brick townhouse. From what Abdon had gathered asking around, the Lehanes were not ranchers, nor homesteaders. They were simply idle rich: old money.

'My name is Abdon Timpson, Miss Lehane. As a matter of fact . . .' Abdon was not exactly certain how to put it. 'This Balam could be a relation of mine. May I come in?'

Janet looked startled, but before she could answer, a

coarse bellow thundered from within the house. Abdon looked over Janet's shoulder to see an elderly man approach. His wizened face and thin wisps of whitened hair on an otherwise bald head suggested a great age. Lacking a leg, the old man strode the marble floor on crutches. Nevertheless, he moved with power and menace.

'Let him in, Janet,' he roared. 'I got an idea who he is.'

'Mr Lehane . . .' Abdon started, but the head of the household cut him off.

'Follow me into the dining room. Janet – serve us some coffee.'

With a pitiless grace that belied his years, he perched on one leg and smacked Janet on her side with a crutch. The young woman nodded obediently, evidently well-accustomed to such cruelties.

Abdon went after Lehane into his dining room. With a skilfulness that surprised him, Lehane manoeuvred himself into a chair. Abdon sat to the old man's left.

'Look at that, stranger.'

Lehane pointed to a daguerreotype in an ornate frame on the wall opposite. It was rather like a photograph Abdon had once seen of the Texas Rangers. He counted fourteen people in the picture: eight standing on the back row, six on seats at the front. The middle two subjects on the front were Lehane and a woman who may have been his wife. On the woman's right was a little girl, who Abdon guessed was Janet. The others were all boys or young men. The male subjects all wore identical suits, as if they were soldiers in uniform. This was no ordinary family portrait. The figures in the daguerreotype radiated an unspoken ambiance of misery.

One of the little boys in the picture was dark-haired, and

the blemish on his left cheek was unmistakable. The subject was almost identical to photographs of Abdon at the same age. Abdon opened his mouth to speak, but Lehane again interrupted.

'We are a house of God, stranger. Some of those boys are my natural sons. The others are wretches I took in – like young Balam. The Lord chose me to instil discipline in those urchins and bastards, and I did. Calista Richards has served me well. I swear, that woman is doing God's work. But Balam? That boy was born bad. I beat him every single day, and it didn't do any good.'

Janet arrived with a tray of china cups that, with painstaking quiet, she lay on the table. She poured a cup each for her father and his guest. Lehane swiftly drained one cup, then poured himself another. Out of courtesy, Abdon sipped at his cup before spluttering the coffee. It was strongly laced with whiskey.

'Too strong for you, boy? Can't take your drink?' Lehane snorted with undisguised contempt. ' "Stop drinking only water, and use a little whiskey". The book of Timothy, Chapter 5, Verse 23.'

Behind Lehane's back, Janet guilefully wiggled her index finger, beckoning Abdon to follow her.

'Sir, I'll just see if Janet needs a hand.'

He tailed her into the kitchen, glad to get away from the madman at the dining table. Out of earshot, Abdon whispered to Janet.

'Is it OK to talk?'

'That coffee and whiskey will keep him happy for a time. I knew Balam was adopted, but I never knew he had a twin.'

'What can you tell me about him?'

Janet smiled, and Abdon was taken aback to see her face light up.

'Balam was a sweet boy. He was the youngest of the Lehanes. Some of the older boys picked on him, but I wouldn't stand for it. He was a very clever young man. Balam never took to the schoolhouse, but he was good with numbers. He would have made a good bookmaker or pawnbroker, but . . .'

Intrigued, Abdon pressed her. 'Please go on.'

'Balam was a naughty boy. He was always in trouble with Daddy or his teachers. It was little stuff. Wisecracking, cheating in tests, fights with other kids. Nothing serious until . . .'

'You can tell me, Janet.'

'A few years ago. A bank robbery. Balam had only just left school, and fell in with some real bums. They'd go out drinking and stirring up trouble. A gang of masked men held up the Cowbridge bank, but the law caught one of them. He squealed and named his partners, including Balam. Now this culprit was desperate, and I think he named Balam just to try and save his neck. I don't think Balam had anything to do with it, but Daddy . . .'

Janet was interrupted by the snap of crutches on the floor tiles.

'But Daddy had a word with the judge,' Lehane growled. 'He and I are old college friends. I told the justice about Balam, about how he was born out of sin. Told him that a stretch in prison would be good for him. And sure enough, Balam was duly tried and convicted.'

Evidently proud of his meddling, Lehane grinned through yellowed teeth. The whiff of whiskey was pungent.

'He's been in Blackmill territorial prison for some three

years now,' said Janet. 'I'd go and visit him, except . . .'

Abdon noticed that Janet was seething.

'Except I forbid her to leave my house unescorted,' Lehane added. 'So why are you here, stranger?'

'I'm from Bethesda. There were two murders there, and the suspect was a dead ringer for me. Only just learned that I was taken in as a baby. Calista Richards directed me to you.'

'Murders, huh? Well, that Balam carried the mark of Cain.'

'No!' Janet shrieked. The anger she had been fighting to restrain exploded. 'Balam is not a killer!'

# CHAPTER 16

With a fire in her gaze that astonished Abdon, Janet snatched a crutch away. Lehane tottered drunkenly on his one leg. He cowered behind a raised hand as Janet barked in his face.

'That boy was innocent, and you knew it! You fitted up your own son.'

She returned the prop, and faced Abdon.

'That doesn't sound like my Balam, Mr Timpson. I suggest you head out to the prison. They might know something there.'

Abdon was about to turn away, when he saw Lehane indignantly and sullenly dragging himself away. He was reluctant to leave Janet in this bedlam. Abdon handed her a business card.

'Janet – if you need anything, get in touch.'

'When you find out about Balam, let me know.'

As Janet saw Abdon to the door, he noted the look of resolve and strength in the woman's face. Abdon could not imagine the nightmare of living in such a madhouse. Janet, though, was plainly a survivor.

Seeing off her odd visitor, Janet felt saddened. She had

missed Balam dearly. Abdon was so similar to him that it was uncanny. Not only his physical resemblance and birthmark, but his mannerisms and gestures. While Abdon had been polite during his visit, Janet sensed his aura of self-confidence. Abdon was bold, impulsive and charming – just like his twin.

Her father would now limp up to his study, where he would drink whiskey and read aloud from the Bible. Depending on how intoxicated he grew, Janet may or may not see him for supper.

It was only Janet and her father left, now. Mommy had died when Janet was a young girl. Janet recalled her as a kind, loving woman. She and her brothers would flee from their father's scolding to her warm arms. Mommy had been a foil to Daddy's inane rants and drunkenness. Her father's temper and unforgiving ways had driven her to an early death, though.

Janet was the second youngest, but she had grown into the role of a mother figure of sorts for the whole brood. She would robustly endure the backhands of her father, but when he struck one of her brothers, Janet was as protective as a lioness.

She was particularly protective of Balam. He had been the runt of the Lehanes. Though she was only a few years older than him, Janet could still remember the day when Calista had delivered that beautiful baby boy with that odd blotch on his face. Then, Janet had imagined that the blemish was something magical. Sure enough, she and Balam had grown to share a special bond.

Balam had had such a cheek. When Daddy had caught Balam stealing a tot of whiskey, Lehane had dragged him away for a strapping. Janet had feared for her baby brother, but – thrown over Daddy's shoulder – Balam had given Janet a thumbs up and a wink. During the hiding, Balam had refused to give his father the satisfaction of hearing him cry out. The brash defiance had only inspired Lehane to make the thrashing worse. Balam had finally emerged from the study almost unable to walk. Janet had embraced him.

'You alright, Balam?'

Though he had been fighting to hold back his tears, Balam was outwardly beaming.

'Nothing I can't handle, sis.'

As the young Lehanes had grown into adults, they had started to realize that there was something bizarre about their upbringing. Daddy had made no secret of the fact that some of his children were adopted. However, he terrorized all of them with equal brutality. Lehane would march them through Cowbridge in their uniform. The young Lehanes could sense the townsfolk keeping their distance from the family of oddballs.

You could 'Drink your whiskey with a joyful heart' (Ecclesiastes), but 'Do not get drunk on whiskey' (Ephesians). When Daddy misquoted the good book, it all depended on his mood. Janet had never quite understood what had happened to Daddy's leg. Lehane had left the house with two legs one day. He had later returned insensibly drunk with only one. Men from town had carried him home on a stretcher. Daddy had explained the accident but his account had been rambling and nonsensical.

The loss of the limb did not temper his viciousness: 'If thy right leg offend thee, pluck it out' (Matthew). Possessed of an uncanny inner drive, Lehane had continued to hound his children. Indeed, since the accident, his drinking and harshness worsened. Lehane had seemed to realize, though, that he could not chase his brood on one leg indefinitely. Starting with his eldest, Lehane had made arrangements to send his sons away one by one. Calling in favours from his wealthy friends and relatives, he had exiled his sons to other territories and other countries. Ostensibly setting them up with jobs, Lehane had in truth been growing too old and weak to bully the young men any more. The boys had been glad to escape.

Balam had been the naughtiest, and the youngest. He had not been so easy to pack off on a wagon train to Oregon. Lehane had had no idea whether Balam had had something to do with that bank raid. Nevertheless, Lehane had effortlessly convinced himself that jail would straighten Balam out.

That only left Janet behind. As addled by whiskey as Daddy's brain was, there was an animal cunning behind those bloodshot eyes. He knew that he would need a nursemaid as he aged. Moreover, Lehane would also need somebody to belittle and beat. He had pulled strings making it impossible for Janet to wed, nor even find a job.

Janet had long sensed that Daddy was trapping her. She had no designs on his wealth. Daddy had in any case written his children out of his will many years ago. Janet had been crafty, though. She had been setting aside a few cents from her housekeeping money, patiently saving for the railroad ticket to Topeka. Janet was nearly there now, only a few more pennies from freedom.

She was about to clean up the Irish coffee from the dining room when there was another thump at the front door. Janet opened up to find that her visitor had returned.

'Back so soon?' she quizzed.

Janet was a little puzzled when the house caller withdrew a Colt from his jacket.

# CHAPTER 17

'Sheriff' was only a shorthand description for Wood's job. The councilmen who had appointed him called him an Officer of the Peace. Wood was responsible for much more than chasing horse thieves and locking up drunks. When there was a land dispute, Wood mediated. If a Bethesdan was wounded in a gunfight, but lacked close family, Wood had to make sure that the casualty had a safe place to stay and convalesce.

If there was a double murder, and nobody to claim the body, Wood had to arrange the funerals. The sheriff had heard that, in other towns, a man shot dead might be buried in a thin grave on the very spot where he fell. Wood wanted better for Lizzie Adams and Alice Bale. As retiring as the women had been, they had been highly regarded for their warmth and kindness. Wood knew little of their backgrounds, but was resolved to ensure that they were interred with decency.

Therefore, at dawn on Thursday, Wood was awoken by a pounding on his door. The sheriff had paid Gabriel to call on him. Wood occasionally approached the tramp with odd jobs. Gabriel was a drifter and derelict, but Wood had always found him hard-working and reliable. Despite his circumstances, Gabriel was always relentlessly cheerful. The down and out would not shirk from the ugly task ahead of them: digging two graves.

Indeed, as the lawman and tramp strolled towards the churchyard, Wood found Gabriel's energetic chatter a little irksome. Glad as Wood was that he could be assisted by such a keen helper, the lawman was not in any mood for conversation. Wood responded to Gabriel's chat with nods and inarticulate grunts.

The sun seemed to be reluctant to rise that morning. Its lacklustre rays gave the frost the purple sheen of dying violets. But for the cracks and scratches of their shovels on the stony earth, the cemetery was silent. The chilled air stung Wood's nose as he laboured. He exhaled, billowing ghosts of breath. Their stiffened limbs made their efforts all the more testing.

'That'll do, Gabriel.'

The tramp had persevered red-faced through their task. When the graves were ready, Wood relieved his assistant. The sheriff thanked Gabriel with an appreciative pat on his back. Wood thrust five dollars into Gabriel's hand. The lawman had promised him only one. Wood recognized the flicker of indignant pride in Gabriel's eyes, and spoke before the tramp could object.

'Keep it, Gabriel,' he urged, closing his hands around Gabriel's fist. 'You worked mighty hard today.'

Swallowing his affronted pride, Gabriel only nodded.

'Sheriff – mind if I stick around for the funeral? I never knew Lizzie well, but Alice was always powerful nice to me.'

Wood agreed, touched by Gabriel's concern. The lawman was not expecting many people to attend. Lizzie and Alice had been recluses. This odd coincidence had been playing on Wood's mind. Two shy women apparently slain by the same gunman. Yet, Lizzie and Alice were not connected. Were they?

The funeral was held later that day. It would be a simple ceremony. The Goughs had known Lizzie as well as anybody, but she had still been very much a stranger to them. They had sent Ma Gough to represent them at the interment: her husband and boys could not leave the fields.

The mourners observed the funeral in a respectful hush. It was presided over by Reverend Andrews. The preacher was a young man, with a touch of the favourite nephew about him. Though he said very little about the women, his sweet words and prayers were moving. The funeral-goers were saddened by the loss of two such gentle women, and dearly wished they had known them better.

After the proceedings, Wood and Gabriel returned to the graveside. They intended to make rapid work of returning the soil to the open graves. Perhaps because the day's ghoulish labours had been so demanding, Wood had not noticed the grave next to Lizzie's. It was in the name of Zofia Adamski. The dates on the headstone suggested that she had died was she was only a child.

Intrigued, Wood excused himself to Gabriel and dashed into the church. Andrews was within, sat in a pew in prayer.

'Sorry to interrupt, Reverend, but I do need to ask. What can you tell me about Lizzie and Alice? And what about that Zofia girl buried next to them?'

Earnest and patient, Andrews was pleased to help. He led Wood back into the private office in the rear of the church. There, he withdrew some mouldy old papers from a cabinet.

'I was only posted here a couple of years ago, Sheriff. I did not know Lizzie and Alice well.' Andrews spoke in crisp, sharp tones. He would have made a good attorney. 'They were regular faces at church, though. From things they said and a little deduction, I learned a thing or two about them. They were in fact sisters. Zofia was Lizzie's daughter. She died of an illness when she was very young. I do not know the details. This tragedy seemed to change the family. They had been very close, once, but Zofia's death had its impact. Even though they were siblings, in recent years they were like strangers. There was no animosity, but it was like they were dead on the inside. They asked to be buried next to one another. When Alice lost her husband, they only seemed to grow sadder still.'

Wood had known none of this, but it made sense. Both Lizzie and Alice, as outwardly kind as they had been, both seemed to have carried a secret inner sadness.

'Were they Polish? I never heard them speaking Polish, and they never had foreign accents.'

'Yes, Sheriff. Elbieta and Alicja Adamski were their real names. They settled here in Kansas when they were only children. Even though they grew up in America, I believe that they were very traditional in private.'

Wood thanked Andrews. It seemed that Bethesda hid secrets, but the lawman would have to investigate how they were linked to the sisters' murders.

The reverend led Wood back through the church, pausing for a moment to inspect the collection tray.

'Somebody's been generous!' Andrews exclaimed.

Five dollar bills rested on the metal plate. Wood rushed

outside to the graveyard. The sheriff found that the open graves had been replenished with soil, but there was no sign of Gabriel.

# CHAPTER 18

Abdon did not know how much further his investigations would lead him. He would ride out to Blackmill Territorial Prison in the morning. However, the serpentine trail of slime that Calista and his parents had oozed seemed to meander onwards and onwards. Prudent of conserving his dwindling cash, Abdon decided to make camp under a tree. He bought a blanket in the Cowbridge drugstore. After a cheap bowl of soup complemented by a soggy lump of bread, at sunset Abdon shivered under his shawl beneath a tree.

The icy airstream wailed. Abdon watched the sky darken from a dirty winter grey to blackness. Only the wispy jaundice of streetlamps lit the deserted streets. Over the chatter of his teeth, Abdon could barely detect the faint sounds of laughter from a saloon somewhere. The coarse blanket gave Abdon little shelter as he pulled it close to his body.

He knew that, home in Bethesda, a warm house with pressed sheets was there for him. His parents had urged him to stay. Abdon had personally chosen to steal away on this impetuous and ill-planned expedition. With nobody to chat with, and no saloon music to lose himself in, Abdon could only dwell.

He had learned that his natural mother had been an impoverished Pole. Abdon had glimpsed the Lehanes' incubation chamber for madness. These could have been alternative pathways that – but for providence – he might have taken.

'Am I spoiled?' he asked himself.

As shocked as he had been, his impulsive destruction of his father's study now seemed like a childish tantrum. The last couple of nights in dank hotel rooms had been unpleasant enough. Quivering under the bare elm, though, Abdon wondered whether he was cutting off his nose to spite his face. He rolled over and over, but the Arctic ground beneath him seemed to suck the heat from his bones.

Though he was exhausted, the pervasive chill made him restless. After a time, Abdon found himself sitting up against the tree, the shawl hugged close to his chest. Unconsciously, he had drawn Halbert's Colt. Abdon knew little of guns, and could barely operate one. He repeatedly thumbed and released the hammer, as if the weapon were a plaything.

Abdon stared into the darkness, his eyes vacant. He longed for the sweet release of sleep, but the insidious cold would not let him settle. Wakeful yet in a daydream state, Abdon glowered blankly into the gloom.

A distant, yet rapid, slapping sound roused Abdon. He could hear unintelligible human voices. In the darkness, Abdon could barely discern the shadowy figures sprinting down Cowbridge's street. Three shadows stopped under the sickly yellow of the streetlamp. Intrigued, Abdon watched for a few moments.

It seemed as though the men were in an altercation. As the silhouettes danced violently under the lamp, Abdon tried to guess what was happening. It seemed to him that two men were brutally accosting a third. The punches and kicks of the assailants were so furious that, even at the other end of the street, Abdon could hear the sickening cracks and pained cries.

In Bethesda, Abdon would have ignored a punch-up amongst a gaggle of low-lifes. Such fights were not common back home, in any case. Sheriff Wood protected the peace with an invisible, almost omniscient presence. Even tonight, there was no reason for Abdon to intervene. If he felt like playing the Samaritan, Abdon could always knock on a few doors until he found the local marshal.

His encounter with Halbert had emboldened him, though. Indeed, since his parents' revelation, a venomous rage had been simmering in Abdon's gut. Meeting Calista and Lehane had only angered him still more. With stiff fingers, he loaded six bullets into the Peacemaker's chambers.

The .45 in hand, Abdon made no effort to conceal the revolver. Indeed, he made a show of swinging his gun arm as he calmly walked up the street to the combatants. Nearing the disturbance, one assailant nudged the other and nodded towards the approaching stranger. They were heavyset men, no doubt cowboys. The two attackers had a snarling, feral air about them. They eyed Abdon with amused contempt.

Their victim, cowering on the ground, was clearly a small man and little more than a weakling. His face seemed elongated like a coyote's snout. Though the weed's hair had greyed, he may have been a young man. For a second,

Abdon thought the runt had a moustache. He then realized that it was but a square of blood shining black in the darkness.

With an instinct for imminent trouble, the first cowpuncher stepped towards Abdon. He turned a palm to Abdon, imploring him to stop.

'Hold up, stranger,' the cowboy ordered. 'Keep out of this. We're just having a little . . . pow wow.'

The assailant pretended to smile, but his disdain for Abdon was palpable. Abdon noticed the burly cattleman's eyes flickering and Abdon could almost read his mind. The cowboy was keeping an eye on Abdon's Colt, but at the same time could not resist peeking at Abdon's weird birthmark. Behind him, the second cowboy crossed his arms and fixed Abdon in a deliberate show of solidarity with his partner.

'Sir,' Abdon said with deadly seriousness. 'Your friend here's got the message. How's about leaving him be and heading home?'

Infuriated, the cowboy's chin trembled. This irksome stranger was a skeeter that needed to be slapped to bloody mush. He took an angry pace towards Abdon, but Abdon had already predicted the assailants' next move. Before the cowboy could strike, Abdon raised the Colt and hammered its butt down on the cowboy's brow. The bite of the gunhandle made the cowboy collapse to his knees. He wondered for a second why his eyes stung, then grasped that they were full of blood.

'Don't!' Abdon had anticipated the other cowboy's intervention. As the cowpuncher's hand reached for his own gun, Abdon raised and pointed his revolver. The cattleman froze.

'Take your buddy and get out of here.' Abdon gave his order masterfully, without raising his voice. The cowboy helped his bloodied partner to his feet, and led him away into the gloom.

Abdon turned to the wretch lying terrified in the mud. He put his revolver away, and reached down to give the unfortunate a hand up. The little man, though, shook fearfully as Abdon extended an arm to him.

'Please don't hurt me, Balam,' he whimpered.

# CHAPTER 19

Abdon was about to correct the little man, but then decided to play along. Perhaps he could glean some useful information.

'I'm not going to hurt you. What's your name again? I've been away a long time.'

'Irving,' the wretch stammered timidly. 'Irving Price. Don't you remember me? I'm so sorry, Balam.'

'Get up, Irving.' Abdon reached down to offer Irving a hand up. Irving apprehensively took Abdon's hand and staggered to his feet. The smell of whiskey on the man's breath was pungent.

'You live around here? How about putting me up for the night?'

Irving seemed perplexed, but also delighted that he could be of use.

'Sure do, Balam. Renting a little place right around the corner. Heck, after what I did, it's the least I can do.'

Abdon nodded and patted Irving on the shoulder. He was keen to encourage the runt to talk, but was mindful of saying too much. As Irving led the way, his paces were unsteady and drunken. Abdon had to steady the man a few times as he nearly tripped.

'So what was that all about, Irving? Friends of yours?'

'A misunderstanding at the poker table. Those two cowboys thought I cheated them out of a few bucks,' Irving slurred.

'Did you?'

'Yep.' Irving smiled smugly.

They arrived at Irving's place. Irving lit an oil lamp, and through the shadows Abdon caught a glimpse of his new friend's home. It was a tiny bedchamber. Ragged clothes were strewn over the floor. Filthy plates and cups were piled in a washing bowl full of grey water. Irving muttered nonsense to himself as he warmed up some coffee on a sooty stove.

Abdon sat down on Irving's unmade bed. That bare tree and his thin blanket outdoors now seemed inviting. Abdon was curious, though. Irving had mentioned being sorry, and had referred to something he had done. Abdon wanted to know more.

Irving handed Abdon a tiny mug of coffee. The cup was rusty, and Abdon was loath to drink from it. For appearances, though, Abdon took a sip. The coffee was bitter and tepid. There were particles of something floating in the liquid, but Abdon did not think they were grains of coffee.

Knowing that he might reveal his true self, Abdon took a risk.

'Tell me what happened, Irving. It's been a while. I'm not angry.'

Irving joined Abdon sitting on the bed, and sighed. He stopped trying to maintain his façade of conviviality. Irving looked at his feet wistfully, and took a loud gulp of coffee. He began his account. Irving rambled and reminisced, but Abdon divined a few things about Balam.

After being thrown out of school, Balam had drifted from job to job. He had never been lazy. Rather, Balam had repeatedly angered his bosses with his arrogance and belief that he always knew the job better than they did. Between getting fired, Balam would mooch off his adoptive father and make money at the cards table. Balam had a head for figures. He would never take silly risks, but quit when he was ahead. Intelligent and perceptive, Balam could also sniff out cheats.

It was in the saloons and poker dens that Balam had met Irving's gang. Irving said they were 'his' gang, but Abdon read between the lines. He was a weakling too fearful to walk away from bums that bullied and manipulated him.

Balam, it seemed, had been friendly with this gang. His big mouth and taste for whiskey had caused a number of brawls. Balam and his new friends had spent a few nights in the jailhouse.

They had been petty crimes, though. Balam had earned a few dollars here and there: enough for a few beers. His gang, though, had been losers and wastrels. When they finally ran out of cash, they had concocted the raid on the bank.

Balam had emphatically opposed the idea. When his buddies had explained their plan, Balam had laughed out loud. He had pointed out all the flaws in the scheme, and urged his gang not to carry on. Balam had stressed that he wanted no part in it.

Unfortunately, Balam's gang were not reflective types and had not heeded his advice. During the botched bank robbery, nobody was injured or killed. Though the thieves had worn masks, everybody knew who had done it. The gang had been boasting about their upcoming ploy for a while.

The robbers might have escaped, though, had Irving not stumbled during the getaway. No legendary outlaw, Irving had fallen from his horse while the gang fled. His ankle broken, he had still been screaming in agony when the lawmen had literally dragged him to jail.

The thieves had been hunted down and locked up. Balam had been guilty by association. While he had affirmed his innocence, Balam had loyally refused to implicate his friends.

Irving, though, had squealed. The lawmen had sensed that Irving was a weak spot in the gang. After a grilling in the sheriff's office and an extrajudicial hiding, Irving signed the confession that the lawmen had drafted for him. This statement had named Balam as a conspirator. Irving was released as a reward for his cooperation, but his old gang had been transported to Blackmill Prison.

'I'm so sorry, Balam.' Irving was weeping now, and pathetically wiping his snot on the back of his sleeve. 'They beat the heck out of me. I didn't know your name was on the confession. I can't even read, darn it.'

Irving had betrayed Balam. This wretch had willingly taken part in a robbery, yet spilled his guts when he stupidly allowed himself to be captured. Despite the circumstances, Abdon felt a touch of pity for him. A weak man, Irving was not equipped for the criminal way of life into which he had sleepwalked.

Abdon put his arm around him.

'All in the past, Irving.'

Abdon found himself liking what he heard about his long-lost brother. Balam, it seemed, had been a tearaway. But could he be a killer?

# CHAPTER 20

The music of roosters roused Abdon at Friday sun-up. He had put Irving to bed, and then curled up among the trash on the floor. Abdon had had to shoo away a couple of rats. He was pleased to slip away before his host came to.

The freshness of the morning air was a relief to Abdon. He inhaled deeply, enjoying the sensation. It was as if the winter air was purging the filth from his lungs.

Abdon was pleased to see the livery was open early. There was no train nor coach out to Blackmill. Abdon did not imagine that the species of men incarcerated there attracted many visitors. At this thought, Abdon smirked. Balam – his own flesh and blood – belonged to that species.

The rent and deposit for the chestnut cleaned Abdon out. A stranger, he had no credit with the liveryman. Nevertheless, Abdon forced himself to smile and shake the liveryman's hand. It was vital to win the man's confidence. Abdon needed that deposit back.

It was not difficult to find the prison. Abdon rode over the grasslands up the hill. From there, it was easy to see the black fortress in the distance. Abdon felt a frisson of apprehension as he approached. Never did he think that he would ever set foot in a prison.

He tied the rented horse to a post outside the entrance. A thick knocker was attached to the vast, main door. Abdon pounded at the entrance. A door built into the main door swung open. Swaggering, a guard stepped out. The jailer was stocky and square-faced. An intimidating figure, the turnkey could not resist laughing contemptuously in Abdon's face.

'Social call, Balam? Dropping in on your old buddies?'

Abdon had dealt with such officious jobsworths before. Nervous as he was, Abdon would need to assert himself. He handed the guard one of his business cards.

'I am the manager of the Bank of Bethesda,' he declared. 'Balam Lehane is my twin brother, sir. Please take me to the warden.'

Astonished, the jailer led Abdon in.

The turnkey guided Abdon through the landings. Blackmill's inmates rushed to the bars of their cells to spy on this unexpected visitor. The sound was a cacophony of coarse insults, pained shrieks and maddened laughter. A nonstop din, it reminded Abdon of the perpetual noise in a sawmill or factory. Among the noise, Abdon thought he could pick out cries of 'Balam! Balam!'

The jailer led Abdon up to the warden's office. After politely knocking on the door, the guard announced him. The warden appeared incredulous, but invited Abdon to sit. He then sent the turnkey away.

'What can you tell me about Balam Lehane, Warden?'

The prison boss sighed. He may have been as burly as a wrestler in his youth, Abdon thought. Now, though, the warden's suit struggled to contain his plump waist.

'Model prisoner. Smart, hardworking, respectful. He could read and write, and he spent a lot of time writing letters or doing paperwork for other inmates. He followed the rules, but . . . well, I guess he had a cheek. Balam would wisecrack and joke around. He was popular, but . . .'

'But?'

'This is a jailhouse, Mr Timpson. Not everybody appreciated Balam's backchat. He suffered some real bad whuppings. Balam was what my inmates call a stand-up con, though. He never snitched on other prisoners.'

Abdon could sense that the warden was a hard man, but also an honest one. The head jailer was speaking candidly. Abdon described the odd murders in Bethesda. The warden shook his head disbelievingly.

'That surprises me. I often wondered why Balam was inside to begin with. He was not cut out for prison. I don't know how the heck he got through it.'

'Where is he now?'

'Crosskeys, a little town not far from here. Balam served three years and was released early for good behaviour. I helped him get a job in Crosskeys, but I have heard nothing for over a year.'

Abdon thanked the warden and shook his hand. The warden responded with a firm grip, but Abdon could feel his unease. The prison head looked like he was shaking hands with a ghost.

Chaperoned by a guard, Abdon was led back across the prison landing.

'Never liked Balam myself,' the jailer explained. 'Real smart alec. Thought he was funny. Reckon it won't be long 'til I see him again.'

Abdon was barely listening, so thunderous was the prison noise. He hardly paid attention as a prisoner was walked the opposite way along the landing by another guard. As the pair crossed on the walkway, though, Abdon felt a pang of disquiet. The prisoner stopped to address Abdon.

'Say, Balam, how you doing?'

The inmate was lean and muscular, yet as pale as bone. He looked emaciated, but there was a black look in his dark eyes. His escort shoved him and cajoled him, but the prisoner would not shift. He body-blocked Abdon as he tried to pass. The jailers roared in his face and prodded him with their batons, but the inmate was as stubborn as a longhorn.

'You're real quiet, Balam. Where's your wisecracks today, huh? There's something real different about you, now.'

As repellent as the prisoner was, Abdon felt a touch of pity as the escort struck him in the face with his nightstick. The blow cracked like the report of a bullwhip. The inmate, though, scowled invincibly. An evil glimmer in his eyes, the prisoner conjured a blade and held it to Abdon's throat.

'Stick with me, Balam. We got some catching up to do.'

# CHAPTER 21

'Take it easy, Bennett,' the escort urged. Though his words were outwardly calm, he could not hide his panic. Abdon noticed the jailer's Adam's apple rising and falling stiffly as the guard took nervous gulps. 'No need for anybody to get hurt. Let our visitor go and this will be over.'

The prisoner Bennett had moved behind Abdon's back. Staring over Abdon's shoulder, Bennett held his shank close to Abdon's neck. The prisoner seemed to control his blade with expert hands. Bennett held the shank just close enough to Abdon's flesh that the slightest trickle of blood was drawn. The prisoner's frightening embrace made Abdon stiffen fearfully. He glanced sideways at his captor with flickering, terrified eyes. Bennett's sunken eyes, shaven head and pallid skin gave him a skull-like appearance.

'No need to get hurt?' Bennett giggled. 'More like yes need to get hurt. Balam here's one of my favourites, officer.'

The prisoner fixed the two guards scornfully. They seemed to be keeping him at arm's length. Bennett shoved Abdon in the back, imploring his captive to walk down the landing. The jailers let him pass, looking each other in the eyes knowingly.

Bennett walked Abdon back to an empty jail cell. The cell was unlocked. Perhaps the prisoner had only just been released from this lockup. The little concrete room was ordered and clean. Yet, the repellent stench in the cell was even fouler than the air on the landing. In the other cells, the prison had become as frenzied as a beehive. The inmates pressed their faces to the bars, desperate to watch Bennett's ploy. Abdon also saw the guards dashing back and forth, their blue uniforms a blur. Gladdened to see their incarcerated peer winning one up on their jailers, the prisoners chanted 'Bennett! Bennett! Bennett!'

Within the cell, Bennett drew Abdon closer.

'Just you and me now, Balam,' he hissed through decaying teeth. 'We got unfinished business, I reckon.'

Outside the cell, a number of guards stood shoulder to shoulder. They were loading handguns, preparing to train their weapons on Bennett and his hostage.

The warden approached the bars to the cell.

'Let him go, Bennett. Don't make this worse for yourself. I've got ten men here ready to open fire.' The head jailer spoke with deadly gravity. If the prisoner did not comply, it was clear that the warden was prepared for a lethal reckoning.

Bennett, though, only sneered.

'I'm doing life without parole, Warden. Got nothing to lose. I'll dice it with a bullet before letting my new toy go.'

Bennett moved his blade from Abdon's neck to his cheek. The prisoner whispered into his captive's ear.

'You won't be so pretty when I'm done with you, Balam.'

Though Abdon was rigid with fear, Bennett's menacing

words activated some innate survival instinct. Abdon grasped Bennett's wrist with both hands. Taken aback, Bennett struggled to claw at Abdon's face. Abdon's grip was as tight as a rivet, though. With a might that Abdon did not know he possessed, he forced away Bennett's shank.

Entangled in a treacherous waltz, the two shuddered as each strained to overpower the other. Desperate, Abdon rocked his upper body forward, then swung it back with venom. The back of his head collided with Bennett's nose. Recoiling from the impact, the prisoner released Abdon as his hands instinctively moved to his face. Bennett dropped the blade.

Bennett wiped the blood from his nose on the sleeve of his prison uniform. Abdon turned to face him, and recognized the look on Bennett's bloodied face. Halbert had shared that aspect of confused frustration. Abdon could almost read Bennett's warped mind. The prisoner was asking himself how he had been bested by such a wimp.

Bennett did not stop to stare, though. The pain in his nose only seemed to craze him even more. With a bestial roar, Bennett launched himself at Abdon. The prisoner grasped Abdon in a headlock. Abdon resisted with strength, though. Hunched over at their waists, the combatants wrestled.

Abdon's head was locked in Bennett's right arm, and he noticed the prisoner reaching for something with his left arm. Bennett was fumbling to seize Halbert's revolver, which was holstered on Abdon's belt. Abdon had fought back against Bennett with ferocity, but he would be a dead man if Bennett got hold of that Colt. Abdon pumped his legs, driving the two of them against the cell wall.

The impact broke Bennett's hold, but the combatants

collapsed to the concrete floor. During the drop, Halbert's six-shooter fell from Abdon's waist. Abdon had earlier loaded the Peacemaker, and by pure chance the .45 did not discharge as it spun across the ground to the other side of the cell.

Their limbs interwoven like a pit of vipers, the fighters tussled. They each tried to push each other away as they scrambled for the gun. Abdon thought that his heart would burst through his chest as Bennett's hand reached the weapon first. Perhaps it was his banker's brain making a calculated gamble when Abdon seized Bennett's discarded shank. Before the prisoner could get to his feet and cock the revolver, Abdon plunged the blade into the back of Bennett's hand.

The prisoner screwed his eyes shut as he wailed in agony. Snatching the Colt away, Abdon noticed that the chant of the other prisoners had changed. Now, they recited 'Balam! Balam! Balam!' Consumed by contemptuous disgust for Bennett, Abdon rose to his feet, readied the Peacemaker and put the barrel to the screaming prisoner's head.

'Quit it, Timpson.'

The warden put his own gun to Abdon's temple. His intervention broke Abdon out of his bloodlust. Abdon felt a little relieved. Had the warden not stepped in, Abdon did not know what he would have done.

# CHAPTER 22

Intrigued by the knowledge that Lizzie and Alice were sisters, Wood had decided to return to Alice's cottage. Nobody but Reverend Andrews had known that the two recluses were kindred. The sheriff wondered what other secrets the women had hidden.

Riding back to Alice's little house on Friday morning, Wood's spine had prickled. The feeling had been akin to stepping on a grave. Looking through Alice's things and paperwork, Wood had felt a touch of guilt. These were private items. But for Alice's murder, the lawman would have had no business nosing through her artefacts.

This sense of shame, though was wiped away when Wood found the letter. Reading through it, the communiqué had revealed nothing. The letter referred to 'troubles' and the 'help' the writer could offer. Wood might not have read anything in to the euphemisms had he not recognized the signature: Calista Richards of White Rock. Reading that name again had made the sheriff shudder.

The lawman had encountered Calista several years ago. A

young woman had come to his office. She had been emaciated and pale to the point of ghostliness. Clearly weakened by some ordeal, she had been delirious. The sheriff had then thought she might be crazed. Though the lady had been babbling, she had repeatedly insisted that 'Calista took my baby'. Wood had found the almost unintelligible accuser to be difficult to believe. However, something had happened to her. Kidnap was a crime to be taken seriously. The lady had shown Wood a business card for Calista Richards, a White Rock midwife. Wood had taken the woman home, then set off to White Rock to investigate.

When he had arrived at Calista's house, the sheriff had found Calista at home with her attorney present. Calista had stonewalled the lawman.

'Ask my lawyer,' she had smugly answered Wood's questions. 'He's advised me not to speak to you. No crime has been committed.'

Infuriated by Calista's simpering refusals and denials, the sheriff had been about to leave. Before he could exit, though, Calista had added a final piece of counsel.

'And I wouldn't bother with that silly girl, again, Sheriff. My attorney's arranged for somebody to . . . speak to her.'

On his return to Bethesda, Wood had found that the troubled young woman had disappeared. The sheriff had never learned her fate. She had had no family to report her vanishing. Though Calista had had an air of secrecy and menace, the lawman had never discovered what had occurred between her and the young lady.

Now, Calista's name had come up again. It had troubled Wood. He had asked his deputy to look after the office for the day, then headed straight to the railway station.

Presently, Wood rode the train to White Rock. He was

reluctant to abandon Bethesda over such a flimsy lead, but his investigator's instinct told him that there was an important connection. Indeed, as the locomotive pulled out of the station, Wood realized that Abdon must have headed to White Rock on Wednesday. This was another important link. The sheriff guessed that Abdon had also learned something about Calista.

During the rail journey, Wood fidgeted impatiently. The sheriff felt every single revolution of the train's wheels. Though it was a relatively short trip, to the lawman it seemed endless. He was anxious to get in Calista's face. This time, lawyer or not, Calista would talk. If not, Wood would march her back to Bethesda in handcuffs.

As the locomotive's brakes squeaked shrilly on the approach to White Rock, Wood was already standing at the exit. There was quite a crowd waiting to board. As soon as the door opened, the sheriff forced his way through the throng. Even though it had been a few years, he could remember the way to Calista's house. Wood recalled that during his last encounter, he had asked the White Rock locals for directions. Everybody had seemed to know the woman, yet nobody had been willing to talk about her.

Wood's feet pounded during the short walk to Calista's. He was hungry for answers, but as he neared the house, he paused. Calista's residence was a fine brick building, and much more expensive than most people in White Rock could afford. This in itself was odd: that a humble midwife could live in such luxury. Approaching the building, the sheriff could not physically see anything amiss. Rather, it was a feeling of dread in his core. Innately, the lawman knew that there was danger in the air.

He took short, cautious paces to the front door. Wood

unbuttoned his holster and gripped the handle of the Uberti within. The door was ajar: it was unlocked, but it had not been forced. Wood tilted his head slightly to listen for any revelatory sounds within. The sheriff could hear the faint bustle of White Rock in the distance, but only silence from within the house.

Wood withdrew the Cattleman, took a deep breath, and kicked the door. It swung inward and thumped against the wall. Within, the ransacked disorder oddly reminded the sheriff of a snow shaker. He recalled that Calista's front chamber had been like a filing room. Now, all of her dossiers had been torn open and emptied. The sheets of paper within littered the floor like a layer of snowfall. From outside, the cold breeze made the pages flutter.

Like Lizzie and Alice's homes, Calista's house had been upended. There was no denying a connection, now. Calista was linked to the murdered women, but how? Moreover, where was she?

'Calista Richards! This is Sheriff Wood of Bethesda. You OK? Where are you?' Wood bellowed. There was no answer.

His two arms holding his revolver before him in a triangle, the sheriff entered the room. His boots crunched as they flattened the layer of papers beneath. The lawman reached the other side of the room. There, the door to the next room was also slightly ajar. Knowing that Calista's intruder might still be hiding, Wood pushed the door open gently with his toe.

In the corridor beyond, Calista lay face-down spread-eagled on the plush carpet. The bullet wound in her back hinted that she had been shot while running away.

# CHAPTER 23

Flanked by two surly guards, the warden led Abdon back to the prison gate. Abdon felt a little like he had as a child when his father had marched him up to his study for a lecture: worried about the imminent dressing down, yet nevertheless smug about whatever act of mischief he had committed.

At the main entrance, a prison officer took the scruff of Abdon's neck and shoved him outside. The jailers were clearly glad to be ridding themselves of this troublesome visitor.

'Timpson,' the warden snapped before closing the door. 'Balam would never have done what you did to Bennett. Even though he was locked up here, he was kinda soft. He was nothing like you, Timpson. Who the heck are you? I can't figure you out.'

The head jailer gave Abdon a perplexed look, and slammed the door shut with a clang.

That final comment had unsettled Abdon. Only moments earlier he had been pleased by the way he had overpowered a dangerous criminal. The warden's words had numbed him, though. Dwelling, Abdon absent-mindedly unhitched his ride and remounted.

When he had returned to Cowbridge, he could scarcely remember the ride back. Abdon had been lost in introspection, contemplating his own behaviour and what he had learned about Balam. Heading back to the livery, though, Abdon remembered to smile politely and thank the owner gregariously. The liveryman seemed charmed by Abdon's courtesy. He took his horse back to the stable and gratefully handed over Abdon's deposit. Abdon tried not to look too relieved, although he was almost desperately grateful. He sorely needed those last few bucks. Abdon's next stop was Crosskeys. He had no idea what, or who, he would find there.

It was a late train ride to Crosskeys. Abdon had strolled around Cowbridge for the rest of the day. He had been careful to avoid Irving, the Lehanes or anybody else. Abdon had hated idling his time, for he was hungry to learn more about his twin. He was still feeling impatient when he boarded the locomotive Friday evening.

The rising shadows without darkened the cabin, which was lit only by the sickly yellow of a gas lamp. There were only a few other passengers in the compartment and each seemed to be a solo traveller sitting in silence. This pleased Abdon, for he was in no mood for chatter. As the train set off, Abdon tried to lose himself in the puff of the engine and the rocking of the wheels. Perhaps he could nod off during the journey. Abdon's belly groaned, though, for he had been forced to preserve his few remaining dollars. His mind also somersaulted over and over again with thoughts of Balam.

From Irving, Blackmill and Janet, Abdon had learned

several surprises about Balam. Like Abdon, Balam seemed very numerate. Abdon had also noted other similarities. He and Balam both seemed to have a certain cheek and mischievousness. While Abdon's adoptive father had always been strict, Fabian had also been patient and encouraging. Abdon's upbringing had been comfortable. He did not know how he would have adapted had he been raised by the Lehanes, or ended up in Blackmill. Balam, it seemed, had reacted to his hardships with a smile and a joke. Abdon wondered how he would have adjusted to such challenges. Indeed, he tended to sulk if he went two weeks without a new bowler hat.

Even Balam's incarceration, it appeared, had been an injustice. Balam's steadfast refusal to rat out his friends, Irving's craven submission to the lawmen, and Daddy Lehane's meddling had all led to his wrongful imprisonment. They had not been together since Calista greedily divided the two brothers at their birth. Yet, despite the circumstances, Abdon found himself admiring and liking Balam.

Abdon took pause. Balam had been a criminal and a gambler, however petty. As likeable as Balam sounded, there was a killer prowling Bethesda. This murderer's description matched Balam's. Could his twin have a dual nature?

This idea made Abdon feel uncomfortable, for it caused him to think about his own recent behaviour. Abdon had always believed that he merited his haughtiness through his brains, flair and good looks. His arrogance had occasionally provoked fisticuffs that Abdon had talked his way out of. He had never been a violent man, yet, he had petulantly wrecked his father's office. Abdon had twice overpowered Fat Halbert, saved Irving from a beating, and come close to pulling the trigger on Bennett. Perhaps Abdon's violence had been caused by desperation, or his extraordinary circumstances. Alternatively, it was possible that the happenings had awoken some dormant brute in Abdon. If Abdon had a violent side, perhaps Balam did, too.

'Beef jerky?'

Startled, Abdon jolted in his seat. It seemed that he had dozed off for a while after all. A stranger had sat down on the seat opposite him and was offering Abdon a strip of preserved dried meat. Abdon would have been content to carry on absorbed in his ruminations, but he was very hungry.

'Don't mind if I do, partner. Much obliged.'

Abdon tore off a piece, which he chewed gratefully. The stranger was a smartly dressed man of perhaps fifty. His lean physique and dyed black hair made him look much younger. The stranger regarded Abdon with curious, yet cautious, eyes.

'Headed into Crosskeys?'

'Yes, partner.' As taciturn as Abdon felt, his inner businessman instinctively switched on his charm and good manners. 'Family stuff. Most tedious. How about you?'

The stranger had the dour air of a military man, or perhaps a Pinkerton. Abdon could sense that, as ostensibly friendly as Beef Jerky was, the stranger was not a man to be trifled with.

'Department of Corrections. There's a project going on in Crosskeys finding jobs for ex-cons. Kind of like a work gang. I'm an inspector on the project, visiting to keep an eye on things.'

Abdon reached out to shake Beef Jerky's hand. This stranger could help him find Balam.

# CHAPTER 24

Beef Jerky's real name was Kasper Lynch. He had been a prison guard himself before rising to his current position. Abdon found him very easy to talk to. Despite his stern demeanour, Lynch was friendly and kind. His presence was also reassuring. Abdon felt safe around Lynch.

It was late when the train pulled into Crosskeys. Abdon followed Lynch to his hotel, where Abdon was relieved to learn that there was a vacancy. He invited Lynch to join him for a drink at the bar. Lynch accepted. A bachelor who was always on the move, Lynch seemed a touch lonesome.

Having childishly walked out on his parents with nowhere to go, Abdon himself had been feeling lonely the past few days. He was glad of Lynch's company. Lynch spoke in coarse, gravel tones. They made small-talk over a couple of beers, before Lynch came directly to the point.

'What's on your mind, Abdon? I get the feeling that you're pussyfooting around something.'

Lynch's bluntness took Abdon aback. The prison inspector was a no-nonsense man. Abdon felt that he could trust Lynch. Indeed, Lynch had rightly sensed that Abdon had a favour to ask. Abdon shared the full truth with

Lynch. He could scarcely believe the words coming out of his own mouth.

'So I need to ask a favour,' Abdon concluded. 'Can you help me find Balam? If he's even here.'

Lynch seemed thoughtful. He took a long swig of his beer before responding.

'That's a crazy story, Abdon. After thirty years in the prison service, though, I've developed a nose for liars. I'd be glad to help – if I can. Meet me in the lobby at first light.'

The men shook hands again before heading to bed. Abdon felt a great sense of relief. It had been cathartic to discuss his plight, and heartening to find somebody willing to help.

Abdon slept well, and woke feeling refreshed and energetic. At dawn, he found Lynch at the hotel entrance ready for the day. The prison inspector led them to two horses hitched outside.

The gentle hills surrounding Crosskeys were still black silhouettes against the violet skies. Dawn's hush was broken by Lynch's commanding voice.

'We'll ride out to the work camp. It's not too far.'

Abdon held his jacket tight. His body was rigid under the morning cold, and he stiffly mounted up. The chill did not perturb Lynch in the slightest, though. He was a man of granite.

They set off at a gentle canter. Lynch began to describe the work camp. His years as a prison guard had toughened him, he explained. Lynch had watched over killers, thieves and outlaws. Many of the men inside had been rotten, and Lynch was glad that they were locked up. Still others were merely lost souls: young men with no discipline. Lynch had suggested a programme where the prisons found jobs for convicts. Keeping them busy would keep them out of trouble. Lynch had been stunned when the Kansas authorities had acted on his ideas, and honoured that he would be a leading figure in the scheme.

Though Lynch was unmarried, Abdon found that there was something fatherly about him. A career guarding low-lifes and crooks had not corrupted his sense of idealism. Lynch worked tirelessly to offer his wards a new start.

They rode through the fields. On the horizon, Abdon saw tiny white triangles rising from the ground like a line of sails.

'That's the camp up ahead. The men live in tents. It's not well-paid, but the workers are fed and sheltered until they can find something better. The workers dig ditches and irrigation channels for the local farmers.'

They reached the base. There, the tents were empty. A wooden table sat in the middle of the camp. It was covered in dirty crockery.

'There's no guards here, Abdon. The workers are free men. They do their own cooking and washing, and they're free to leave at any time. Let's see if we can find them.'

Abdon could see why Lynch was so keen to help him. Lynch was plainly very proud of the work camp, and wanted to show it off. Abdon could hear shouting in the distance. Lynch led Abdon down the hill.

At the bottom of the hill, Abdon could see a handful of men digging. Though they wore denim shirts and jeans, their work uniforms were muddied and filthy. Against the muddy hills, their garb had an almost camouflage effect. As dirty as their work was, the men seemed to be in high spirits. They joked, laughed and chatted as they toiled.

'Let's stop here a moment, Abdon. I'll call the foreman,' Lynch instructed. 'Jake!' he bellowed. 'Come up here! We got a visitor!'

A worker lay his spade down and jogged up the hill. Jake was a redhead with a thick, fiery beard. Hours of hard labour every day had developed his muscles. The foreman was powerfully built. As he reached Lynch, Jake eyed Abdon with suspicion. Abdon swallowed nervously.

Jake nodded politely to Lynch then carried on scowling at Abdon.

'Abdon, this is Jake Cody Bowe, the foreman here. Jake, this is Abdon Timpson. It's a crazy situation, but Abdon is looking for his twin brother Balam Lehane. Is he here, Jake?'

His face flushed, Jake wiped his sopping brow, streaking it with mud. The foreman looked incredulously from Abdon to Lynch and back. It was as if Jake could not quite believe the situation.

'Respectfully, Mr Lynch, but is this some kind of joke?' Jake panted. He spoke in serious, distrustful tones, and palpably resented the odd visitor's interference. 'Because Balam Lehane is dead.'

# CHAPTER 25

Lynch had a sense for a volatile situation. Jake plainly resented Abdon's presence. Abdon seemed nervous and uncomfortable. The foreman's revelation had only made the atmosphere tense. Lynch needed to speak up.

'OK, boys. Let's head back to the tents. Maybe we can get to the bottom of this. Come on.'

Jake shot Abdon a poisonous glance, but begrudgingly followed Lynch back to the camp. Abdon was dumbfounded. A maelstrom of thoughts and emotions twirled in his head. Dumbstruck, Abdon silently walked back with the prison inspector.

'Sit down, Abdon.'

Lynch implored Abdon to take a seat at the camp's dining table. It was more of an instruction than an invitation. Jake busied himself preparing a pot of coffee. Abdon watched the foreman uneasily as Jake ground the java beans with a venomous glimmer in his eyes. Jake reminded Abdon of a rattler coiled to strike at the merest provocation.

Lynch approached Jake and lay a fatherly hand on his

shoulder. Clearly, Lynch held no fear of his passionate foreman.

'Jake, what can you tell us about Balam Lehane? Abdon here has been trying to track him down.'

Lynch's calming words did nothing to reassure Jake.

'Mr Lynch, sir, with respect,' the foreman spat. 'We worked with Balam for six months. He was a real good guy: hard-working, honest, funny. We all liked him Then he dies in . . . shall we say odd circumstances? And now his ghost shows up. This . . .' He glowered at Abdon. 'This Timpson fellow is a dead ringer. I don't like this, Mr Lynch. There's something real hooky about the whole affair.'

Jake had no doubt been a prisoner himself. Abdon noted, though, that he was articulate and persuasive. There was a real intelligence behind those blazing eyes. Abdon noticed that Lynch was looking at him, as if prompting him. He took the hint, then explained the background to his search for Balam.

Abdon's account seemed to pacify Jake. He listened carefully, even serving Abdon and Lynch cups of coffee. Abdon took a sip of the scalding drink. He was surprised by how fine the coffee was. Despite being an ex-con up to his knees in muck every day, Jake possessed some skill in the kitchen.

'Sure is crazy stuff, Mr Timpson. But I'm nobody's fool. I can tell you're truthing.'

'Will you tell me about Balam? How did he die?'

Jake had been at the work camp for three years. Lynch had noticed his brains and work ethic. Jake had then been appointed as the foreman. The job paid a pittance, but it was infinitely better than life on the inside. Jake had grown to enjoy the work; he was tough on his charges. Jake would lead the digs with a blistering pace. The wasters and whingers who could not keep up were sent packing. Some of them ended up back in jail, others stayed at the camp for months or years.

Jake had sensed that Balam was a grinder. The young man was slightly built, and also something of a clown. Balam had found the work hardy. When Jake barked his orders, though, Balam had never complained. He had not been physically the strongest, but Balam had persevered. His humour had also made him popular with the men. Jake could detect that – like him – Balam was determined not to go back to jail.

The foreman constantly reminded his troops that they were free men. They worked around a rota that Jake wrote.

'But just because you're free doesn't mean I won't fire you if you don't shape up,' Jake would add. Fighting, drinking or other trouble-making were sacking offences.

Their meagre wages meant that they could ill afford a night at the saloon, nor the house of ill fame. On their days off, the men would chip in for a bottle of whiskey. They would sit around the fire sharing sips of the liquor while they joked and ate a mess of beans.

Jake recalled, with great clarity, the last time he saw Balam alive. It was an April night some six months ago. The workers had been enjoying their night off around the campfire. Though spring was then imminent, there had been a chill in the air, and the men had welcomed the fire's warmth. While the skies had greyed, the flickers of flames had cast a golden glow. The fire crackled, but its sound was masked by laughter and song. Jake had been chewing the last scrapes of his supper. Though he was outwardly strict and forceful, the foreman had grown to enjoy life on the camp. Many of the men, including Jake himself, were estranged from their families. The work camp was a surrogate brotherhood where the brethren worked and lived together, watching each other's backs.

Balam had been as funny as ever that night; his humour had been good for morale. Balam had always been reluctant to talk about his past life and his time in prison. Jake had noticed the signs, though. Balam had scars, telling aches and soreness. The lock-up had been an ordeal for Balam. Joker though he had been, Balam had been one tough customer.

'Excuse me, gentlemen,' Balam had announced with a grin. 'Too much firewater and now I have to fire out some water.'

The men had laughed. Balam was forever making such silly gags. Merry but not intoxicated, Balam had creeped out into the darkness to relieve himself. The ditches also doubled as latrines.

It was the final time Balam had been seen alive. After a while, Jake had sent out men to find Balam. It had not taken them long. He was discovered face down in a ditch, drowned.

Jake was loath to show raw emotion, but Abdon could tell that the foreman was moved. Fighting back tears, Jake insisted that Abdon and Lynch follow him to the corner of the field. There, Jake pointed out a grave marked with a simple wooden crucifix etched with the words 'Balam Lehane'.

'Like I said, there's something real hooky about the whole affair. Balam wasn't drunk that night. And we never heard splashing, or Balam crying out for help. That ditch wasn't even that deep! I just can't figure it out.'

Shocked, Abdon stared at the improvised grave. From the descriptions he had heard of Balam, Abdon had been beginning to doubt that he was the Bethesda killer. Balam had died some six months ago. Who, then, was the doppelganger stalking Bethesda?

# CHAPTER 26

Typically so laconic and charming, Abdon now stood gazing at the humble grave in stunned quiet. Jake noticed Abdon's lips quivering. It was as if he were about to ask a question, but was unable to form the words. The foreman's perception of Abdon had shifted rapidly. Jake had been guarded on first meeting the banker, but he had been impressed by Abdon's sincerity. His testimony had been uncanny, but Jake could see with his own eyes that Abdon was Balam's double.

A dozen emotions thrashed in Abdon's core. He was moved by Jake's palpable affection for Balam. Abdon was also saddened. Everybody had spoken so highly of Balam. Abdon somehow felt as if he had lost a friend. Yet, a fist of fear also clenched within his gut. Abdon's quest had been impulsive and ill-conceived. Still, he had thought that finding Balam would somehow resolve the Bethesda mystery. With Balam long dead, those killings remained unexplained.

Abdon could sense that Jake and Lynch did not know quite what to say. Steeling himself, Abdon took charge.

'I thank you, Mr Bowe, for your time. It's a great shame

I never met Balam, but I guess this is the end of the road.'

Forcing himself to smile politely, Abdon shook Jake's hand and returned to his mount on the hilltop. Lynch sent his foreman back to the dig, and went to join Abdon back in the camp.

Jake could tell that his weird visitor wanted a moment to himself. He waited at Balam's grave as Abdon and Lynch returned to the tents. Lynch had always been dedicated to the work camp. Whenever they had needed equipment, or there was an ex-con making trouble, Lynch had intervened. Lynch was a kind of middle-man between the prisons and the camp. He was very good at keeping the authorities out of Jake's hair. Jake trusted and respected Lynch.

Abdon, too, had won Jake over. It had been upsetting for Jake to relate the facts of Jake's death. There had been one incident, though, that Jake had kept quiet about. At the time, Jake had not dwelled on the event, but now he wondered what the encounter could have signified.

It had been back in April, only a few days before Balam's drowning. Jake and Balam had ridden in to Crosskeys for supplies. Balam, Jake had noticed, had possessed a flair for numbers. Lynch provided the work camp with a modest budget. Balam had supported his boss in managing the fund. He had been conscientious in checking the change from the Crosskeys stores. Balam was also skilled at negotiating credit with the suppliers in town. More than anything, though, Balam had been trustworthy. Though Jake's men were mostly striving to transform their lives, a few of them were thieves and liars. Jake had not been ready to entrust them with cash.

It had been a beautiful spring day. Jake and Balam had

been sitting side by side on the platform of the shaky, third-hand buggy as they had headed into Crosskeys. Their carriage had rocked uneasily and squeaked as it had rumbled over the fields into town. The two had hoped that today would not be the day the buggy finally broke. Memories of their jail cells had not faded from their minds. Today, they could suck deeply on the warm, April air. They were free men, but liberty came with responsibility.

They had had several errands to run; a day in Crosskeys was not a day of leisure. Jake had been mindful of returning to the fields as quickly as he could. After all, Lynch might show up at any time. The foreman had sent Balam to the bank, while Jake had headed to the hardware store.

Jake had been placing an order for a score of shovels. They were the camp's biggest expense. Indeed, each spade endured so much punishment that it was never too long before it snapped. The foreman remembered the hardware store shopkeeper eyeing him cautiously, as he always did. The men from the camp always paid their bills. They were in fact good customers. Crosskeys' locals never quite knew what to make of their ex-con neighbours, though. While Jake's men never stirred up trouble, they had a notoriety that preceded them.

The foreman had paid up and thanked the shopkeeper politely. There had still been much to do. Jake exited the hardware store and passed the saloon.

There, he had paused. Within the drinking den, it had been dank and shadowy. Despite the gloom, though, Jake had noticed a familiar face within. With that distinguishing blemish, there could be no mistake. Sat at the table, with a glass of whiskey before him, was Balam. Their eyes met.

Jake had instantly angered. Balam had been a faithful lieutenant. At times, ladies had made excuses to talk to the boyishly handsome young man with that oddly attractive birthmark. Never had Balam been a shirker, though. Jake had found it disappointing and enraging to spot his right-hand man squandering the cash entrusted to him.

The foreman had taken a furious pace into the saloon, then looked back as a hand had clasped his shoulder.

'All done at the bank, boss. What's next?' Balam had chirped. Startled, Jake had looked back into the murk of the saloon. That stranger with the weird blemish had vanished. Jake had wondered if he was seeing things.

'Balam, did you enter the saloon? Tell the truth, now, partner.'

'No, boss. What's up?'

'Never mind. Let's get moving. Lots and lots of laundry to collect.'

Jake had brushed the sighting from his mind. Wishful thinking. After Balam's inexplicable drowning, Jake had asked himself if there could be a connection. Again, though, he had not dwelled. Jake was not even certain what he had seen in the saloon that day.

Perhaps he should have told Abdon and Lynch. The foreman had hesitated, though. Jake did not want his supervisor to think him a fantasist, nor a madman.

Watching Abdon and Lynch mount up for their return to town, Jake picked up his shovel with weariness and sadness. He climbed the hill, heading back to the dig.

'What did I see that day?' he muttered to himself. 'Probably nothing.'

# CHAPTER 27

Though he knew it was futile, Wood gave Calista's shoulder a shake.

'Calista! Calista! Can you hear me?'

There was no reaction, but the sheriff could feel a tepid heat radiating from the slain woman. This killing had been recent, and perhaps the killer was still nigh. Though it was only the early afternoon, the skies outside were a wintry white. Calista's house was unlit, and its interior grey with shadow. Wood listened carefully, his senses magnified. The slightest breeze without, or the dullest creak of woodwork within, all portended danger. Wood's own wheezing breaths sounded husky and laboured. The lawman could detect the dirty, carbon smell of cordite intermingled with the metallic scent of fresh blood. A gun had been discharged recently. The sheriff had to force himself not to squeeze his own weapon in fear.

The thud came from upstairs. It was hardly a loud report: only the sound of feet shifting stealthily. To Wood, it signalled that the intruder had scrambled upstairs like a startled racoon. Every sinew of the sheriff's flesh tensed. The confrontation was imminent.

He stepped over Calista's body. Like a Viking berserker, he charged up the stairs. The lawman's pounding feet forewarned the interloper, though. Wood did not pause to browse the plush furnishings in Calista's lavish bedroom. As he stormed breathlessly into the chamber, the lawman only saw a silhouette escaping through the window. It climbed away as nimbly as a black tarantula. Instinctively, the sheriff aimed the Uberti and fired. Within the bedroom, the song of the revolver was almost deafening. As rapid as Wood's gun-hand was, the spider had fleetingly dropped out of sight to the ground below.

The metal of the Cattleman hot beneath the lawman's sweaty fingers, he sprinted over to the window to fire again. Thumbing the hammer, the sheriff pointed at the fleeing figure below. Wood squeezed the trigger, and the Uberti thundered once more.

The killer seemed to jolt sideways, somehow sidestepping another bullet through agility or pure fortune. Wood noted that the intruder moved like a young man. The interloper's features were obscured by a Stetson and a bandana around his face. Electrified by the second gunshot, the escaping killer's pace escalated.

Alarmed that he would lose his quarry, the lawman hauled his heavy frame through the window in pursuit. A dull frisson of pain pulsed through his bones as he landed uncomfortably on the grass below. The intruder sped around the corner. Wood's lungs burned. His limbs motored with stiff reluctance, but the lawman was consumed by a hunter's tenacity. He followed.

Calista's house was just outside White Rock. The killer ran out to the surrounding fields. As the sheriff pursued, he noticed his prey glancing back over his shoulder. The lawman recognized that same nervousness from countless arrests. This rat knew that he was cornered.

The interloper was nearly at the other side of the field from his hunter. Wood noticed the killer halt. Though the lawman could only make out the small figure in the distance, Wood rightly guessed what he was doing. He was about to draw on his pursuer.

The sheriff, too, stopped and pulled his trigger. It was not an easy shot, but if the lawman's bullet missed, the killer's might not.

Wood fired. Like a felled tree, his target collapsed to the ground.

The killer lay prone on the grass, his limbs loose. The music of the revolver still echoed over the fields. Though the winter breeze was icy, it felt pleasing on the lawman's soaking flesh. Panting as he approached the fallen burglar, the sheriff licked his dry lips. His throat was parched.

The killer lay dead in a freezing cold field, his gut pierced by lead. Creamy wisps of breath steamed from Wood's lips as he walked up to the dead intruder. He returned the Uberti to its holster, then crouched down to inspect the body. The corpse was clad in black trousers and a black shirt: clearly an experienced housebreaker. Wood pondered what the intruder might have wanted, and whether there was any connection to the Bethesda murders. The lawman reached down to remove the scarf from the body's face.

Had Wood been more careful, he might have noticed that there was no blood on the apparent corpse, no gunshot wound, and that the cadaver was in fact breathing faintly. Before the sheriff could unmask the killer, the corpse raised its gun hand.

Unnerved, Wood pinned the hand holding the Colt back down. He used his other arm to press down on the burglar's neck, but the killer thrashed like a rodeo bull. Though the two combatants were as close as lovers, the killer found enough space to throw a punch with his free hand.

The killer's fist struck forward like a piston. It hit Wood's jaw, and he recoiled onto his back groaning in agony. The pain in the lawman's shattered chin was so piercing, though, that he closed his eyes in misery. Even the torture of a splintered jaw, though, could not distract Wood from the unmistakable click of a Colt being readied.

'Fooled you, lawdog. Playing possum – always works a charm on saps like you.'

The killer's words were coarse, but Wood thought he recognized their arrogant timbre. He looked up, his vision blurred. Wood tried to speak, but he could only gargle due to the hot blood pooling in his mouth.

'Not following you, lawdog. Broken jaw'll do that to you, but I got a good idea what you're driving at. Don't fret. I'll show you.'

With evil arrogance, the killer pulled away the kerchief from his face. Though the features were familiar, Wood knew that it could not be Abdon. The sheriff's brain was still processing this contradiction when it was penetrated by a bullet.

# CHAPTER 28

The nights without Abdon had been depressing for Fabian and Ida. They had known since their son's infancy that the truth would ultimately be exposed. However, the couple had mentally postponed the reckoning. The confrontation with Abdon, though, had been no relief. Fabian would have continued the secrecy were it not for the mysterious deaths of Lizzie and Alice.

Fabian had returned to the bank, and he and Fifield were sharing Abdon's work between them. The two were utterly professional. They were determined to look after the office even during a family upheaval. During the week, the queues at the counter had been long; everybody in town wanted a meeting to see if they could glean some choice gossip. With expert brave faces, Fifield and Fabian had been deflecting the intrusive questions.

'Abdon's out of town on business.'

'That arrest was only a misunderstanding. Sheriff Wood's on the case.'

Fending off such intrusive questions on top of their usual routine had been draining. Yet, when Fabian had returned home exhausted, he had been unable to sleep.

His mind was playing the same images over and over again: thoughts of Abdon's childhood, memories of Calista's deceit, and fears for Abdon's whereabouts.

Fabian and Ida had hardly spoken. At times, the house's miserable silence had been broken by the sound of Ida's solitary sobs. Whenever Fabian had gone to comfort his wife, though, Ida had spurned him with furious screams and spiteful words. Nothing had brought the Timpsons more joy than raising Abdon. They now dreaded that their secrecy had forever ruined this happiness.

Fabian was resolved to carry on, though. He trudged to the bank every morning with haggard, bloodshot eyes. Appearances were everything in banking. Without the confidence of his customers, he was nothing.

Thus, on Saturday night, Fabian insisted that he and Ida keep their booking at José's. Ida wanted to do nothing more than sit in a dark room and brood. Fabian had been resolute, though, and Ida had acquiesced.

The Timpsons dined at José's every Saturday. José and his wife Lesta were good customers to the bank, and Fabian was mindful to give them some business in return. Stepping down from their private stagecoach, Fabian locked Ida's arm in his as they entered the restaurant. Fabian was playing the part of the affable local banker. Ida, with glum resignation, allowed her husband to lead her.

They entered. The waves of warmth inside were pleasing to Fabian's cold bones. José's restaurant was lively and busy. Fabian could sense the diners sneaking glances at the local man drawn into scandal, though. The air hummed with conversation and, in the corner, a mariachi played. Fabian made a show of inhaling the odours of spices and simmering sauces. It would have been an enjoyable night but for the blackness in his core.

José and Lesta came over to their guests. Lesta was always the perfect hostess. She kissed Fabian and Ida on their cheeks and then tactfully discussed the menus rather than Abdon's arrest. Though José's English was faltering, he greeted Fabian and shook his hand. While José was burly and taciturn, Lesta was diminutive and extrovert. In Bethesda, their partnership was a popular one.

Lesta walked them to their seats. Fabian ordered for both of them, but the Timpsons hardly touched their dishes. Ida sat at the table as unspeaking and grey as a statue. Fabian talked to himself and played with his food. He prayed that nobody would sense that something was amiss.

Fabian had instructed his driver to collect him at 9pm. When the hour came, Fabian was glad to leave. The Timpsons boarded their stage for the return to their mansion. Fabian stared entranced at the blackness outside the carriage's window, his mind numb. The Timpsons did not speak during the drive back. Fabian found the clip of the wheels on the frozen ground almost interminable. In winters past, Fabian and Ida would have cuddled for warmth. Tonight, they sat shivering and looking away from each other. Have I lost my son? Fabian asked himself. Have I lost my wife as well?

At the house, the Timpsons alighted. Fabian sent his driver home. He would not be needed. The Timpsons would not be going out tomorrow.

Fabian stepped up to the thick oak door. He reached for the keys in his pocket, then hesitated. Fabian nudged Ida, then pointed at the doorframe. The door had been jemmied open.

Cautiously, Fabian pushed at the door. It was heavy, and opened slowly. Ida was always house-proud, fastidiously attending to the house's good order in person. The muddy footprints on the marble floor were fresh. Along the hallway, tables were overturned and the grandfather clock had been pushed over. The ransacking had been very recent.

Fabian listened intently. An owl hooted somewhere in the distance, but he could not hear any movement within. Fabian held Ida close to him, and entered tentatively. He was struck by the rotten smell within. Ida took meticulous pride in her cleanliness. The odour reminded Fabian of the air in a saloon after last orders. It was a combination of stale cigar smoke, the dregs of whiskey glasses and spilled beer. Whoever the burglar was, he stank.

'Welcome home, Mr Timpson.'

The couple turned around. Hidden behind the door, their interloper had been waiting. The burglar was dressed in black. He was unshaven and unwashed, but that blemish was unmistakeable.

'Abdon!' Fabian gasped.

'No!' Ida scowled. 'That's not my Abdon.' A mother can tell.

The shadow stepped forward and held his weapon to Fabian's head. Though the intruder fixed Fabian with menacing eyes, Fabian met them with defiance.

'Show me where the paperwork is, Timpson,' the burglar snarled. Fabian was taken aback. This repellent creature even sounded like Abdon.

'Just who the heck are you, stranger?' spat Fabian.

'No questions, money man. Get me your papers right now.' Abdon's double poked Fabian on the nose with the barrel of his Colt. 'Or you're dead.'

# CHAPTER 29

Saturday sunset, Abdon once again found himself at the train station. He and Lynch had ridden back into town in despondent silence. Back in Crosskeys, Abdon had forced himself to say goodbye to Lynch with a hearty handshake. His good cheer was a pretence. Lynch could sense Abdon's hidden sorrow.

'Where you headed now, Abdon?'

'Bethesda, I guess.' Abdon's choice of words was telling. Though Abdon had not spoken of the rift with his parents, Lynch could sense that Abdon's house was not in order.

Abdon intended to take the train back. Once he arrived, he did not know what he would do. Part of him longed for his parents' love and affection. Yet, he was ashamed of the rash way he had stormed off. Having scorned their approaches, Abdon was also a little too proud to change his attitude. He was also down to his last couple of dollars. Abdon would need to find a job and fast, or he would be bedding down next to Gabriel in his shack.

'Goodbye, Abdon. I wish I could have helped more.'

Lynch had said his farewell. He then returned to the hotel. He had other work camps to visit. In his profession, he was always on the move. Walking away, Lynch felt a touch saddened. Abdon had been earnest and smart. It was as though Lynch was seeing a friend for the final time.

There were few other travellers on the locomotive that evening. Melancholy, Abdon stared into the darkness outside as the train chugged away. The carriage was freezing. Abdon hoped that the heat from the engine would warm the compartment. He licked his lips. His mouth was bitter and sticky. Abdon had not eaten, nor drank anything since Jake's coffee. He imagined that his parents would be enjoying their usual Saturday night in José's. It was possible that Abdon would be waiting tables there before long.

The train stopped in Cowbridge. Abdon thought once again of the Lehanes. Their home was a madhouse. Abdon reflected how fortunate he was to have been raised by the Timpsons, and not Daddy Lehane.

Another traveller boarded at Cowbridge. The passenger was drunk. Abdon could smell the alcoholic haze before the traveller had even entered the carriage. He was a grossly corpulent man in a white suit. Expensive as his attire undoubtedly was, it was stained by spilled whiskey. As the drunk staggered down the aisle, Abdon caught a closer whiff of him. Beyond the whiskey mist was a revolting pong of sweat and unwashed flesh. Before the drunk could sit, Abdon shot him a repelling glance that signalled that Abdon did not want his company.

The drunk sat opposite another couple, who were possibly a father and son travelling together. Abdon tried to ignore the glutton's slurred boasts. However, he spoke so loudly that the whole carriage was compelled to listen.

The fat man had earlier made a lot of money on the sale of forty head. A cattle baron, he had spent the afternoon celebrating. On another occasion, Abdon might have tried to tempt him over to the Bank of Bethesda. The drunk's manner and words were just as obnoxious as his smell. Abdon, though, was skilled in pretending to like people. Salesmanship had been part of his job.

The hog's bragging continued. His breeches could literally not contain his porcine gut. Yet, apparently he had a pretty, young wife at home and a prettier, younger mistress elsewhere. He was apparently so wealthy that he was bored of business. Soon, he would soon be standing for Congress. The drunk then shared a ridiculous tall story where he had outdrawn a challenger in a duel. This was obviously pure fantasy. The baron's hot dog fingers would never have fitted through a trigger guard.

Indeed, the men sitting opposite the hog could not help guffawing.

'Something funny, partner?' the baron sneered, his false pride affronted.

The younger of the two passengers responded.

'Come on now. That's some story, mister. Maybe you're exaggerating just a little.' He put it as politely as possible.

Enraged, the drunk's already flushed skin reddened still further. Ranting at an even noisier volume, the baron sprayed his audience with a film of spit. His garbled, angry words were indecipherable.

Watching the scene, Abdon could sense danger. After Halbert and Bennett, fat drunks did not frighten Abdon in any way. Abdon lay a hand on his Colt, just in case.

The drunk began clawing at the young man and his father. Abdon was about to step in, but his intervention was unnecessary. The hog was so fat that he could not reach over to grab his tormentors. Indeed, the father and son laughed out loud at the drunk's pathetic efforts.

The son whispered something to his father. Smiling, the two rose from their seats. Together, the couple tugged at the cattle baron's ankles. They needed to heave, but they unseated the drunk. With a clump, his butt hit the carriage floor. Like an upturned crab, the drunk was stuck on his back. The baron grasped wretchedly at the air.

Throughout the compartment, the other travellers applauded and laughed. Abdon joined in. It was a welcome moment of good cheer.

The father and son moved to the seat opposite Abdon.

'Nice work, gentlemen. That dumb ass was asking for it.'

'Thanks, partner. Say, mister . . . have we met?' the son asked.

Abdon did not recognize the men. Naturally, he wondered if the travellers had somehow encountered Balam.

'Do you mean in Crosskeys or Cowbridge?'

'No, mister. No offence, but that birthmark sticks out a little. My pa and I are drovers. We move around a lot, depending where the work is. Back in Bethesda, a man just like you asked for directions.'

'Directions?'

'Yeah. We're from out of town, so we couldn't help. But the man with the birthmark asked how to get to the Timpson place.'

Walking out on his parents, Abdon had left them in peril. That weird doppelgänger was still on the prowl, his sights on Abdon's mother and father.

It was time to go home.

# CHAPTER 30

Abdon was no longer thinking about his childish pride, nor even his parents' apparent deceit. As soon as the travellers had told him about the weird double headed to the Timpsons', Abdon did not think about anything. Like a cougar that had scented blood, he was transfixed. Abdon impatiently paced up and down the train's aisle. He was desperate to return home, every inch of his flesh tingling anxiously.

When the locomotive finally slowed painstakingly into Bethesda's station, Abdon was already at the door. He yanked up the lock and burst out of the exit, the swinging door almost shattering as it clanged against the carriage exterior. Before the conductors could raise their infuriated voices, Abdon had vanished from the station.

He sprinted into the blackness. Abdon's shoes clicked uncomfortably on the frosty ground. The hard impact made his ankles shudder. Abdon ran onwards heedless. Breathless, the wintry air stung his nose and lungs. Abdon tasted salty perspiration thick in his mouth. He somehow knew that his mother and father were vulnerable. They needed their son.

Nearing the mansion house, Abdon noticed silhouettes

darting back and forth against the light shining through a window. Within, there was a disturbance. He prayed that he had reached his parents in time.

Abdon could hear agitated voices within. They were murmurs, but he recognized the timbre of his father's speech. The main door was slightly ajar. Abdon charged at it shoulder first.

Inside, the lobby seemed to wobble. The marble tiles rose to pummel Abdon on his forehead. He hit the ground face first. Dizzied, he tried to turn around. Abdon recognized the frightened gasps of his parents. Confused, he did not immediately identify the stranger who had just tripped him up.

Abdon stared into the all too familiar face: his own. For a man that so adored his own reflection, Abdon found it disconcerting to see his mirror image come to life. He stared mesmerized at his double, and the doppelgänger returned the gaze. Neither could quite believe what he was seeing.

'Abdon Timpson,' the twin growled. 'Heard you running up the drive. Glad you're here. I need you.' The double spoke in a rumble refined by many years of drinking and smoking too much. The voice was otherwise identical to Abdon's. Indeed, had Abdon stopped shaving and bathing for a few weeks, the two would be indistinguishable.

Abdon motioned for his Colt. He paused when the double pointed his own weapon. Fabian took a pace towards the intruder. The doppelgänger swung his revolver back to Fabian.

Despite his fondness for war stories and military collectibles, Fabian was not ordinarily brave. He was kind and dedicated, but no gunslinger nor pugilist. However, to see his son prone on the floor with a gunman standing over him aroused in Fabian a passionate urge to protect.

'Take one step closer, Timpson. I dare you,' the interloper roared.

Fabian did take another pace, and another, and another. When he was within an inch of the intruder, the burglar exploded in fury. He seized Fabian's lapel with one hand, pushing him back against a cabinet with angry force.

The interloper was strong. He shoved Fabian with such cruelty that the impact broke the rifle cabinet. The wood made a whiplash sound as it cracked, while Ida wailed in horror. It disgusted Abdon to see his father humiliated so, but he noted a certain glimmer of defiance in Fabian's eyes.

The air was filled with dirty soot that smelled oddly familiar to Abdon. Fabian's face and clothes were powdered with black dust. Abdon now remembered how he knew that grainy scent. It was gunpowder. The rifle cabinet had contained the Limey.

'Don't even think about it, Abdon!' the double bellowed, spinning around to face him. Abdon had indeed tried reaching for his Colt again while the doppelgänger had been distracted. He froze when the double trained his gun on him.

Behind the doppelgänger, slumped against the shattered cabinet, Fabian writhed. Abdon could not make out what his father was doing, but Fabian was fiddling with something. He could see that look in Fabian's eyes, though. Abdon had been affronted when he had learned that Fabian was not his flesh and blood. This did not matter anymore, though. Fabian was imploring Abdon to do something. It was as if Abdon could read his father's mind. Fabian's eyes were telling him to keep this stranger talking.

'So what do you want, mister? Money? We got plenty. Why don't I take you down to the bank?'

The double seemed to laugh. It was a coarse roar, like an alligator growl.

'Pretty soon, Abdon, that bank is going to be all mine anyways. Where's the paperwork? I want the lot. Deeds, ownership papers, articles of association.'

This perplexed Abdon. The mirror image did not seem to be a man of sophistication. His invasion, though, was much more than a smash-and-grab.

'You don't seem like the corporate type.'

The stranger's face flickered angrily. He resented Abdon's comment. The double kicked Abdon in his flank several times. Abdon yelped as the doppelgänger's pointed boots stung his flesh over and over again.

'Think you're smart, boy? I heard all about you, fancy pants. Hotshot banker. Think you're smarter than me?'

Beyond the intruder, Abdon could see his father continuing to tamper. Fabian carried on glancing at his son. Keep it up, his eyes said. Keep him distracted.

'Why don't you ask me what you really want to ask me, son?' the intruder gloated.

Indeed, the question was so obvious, yet incredulous, that Abdon could scarcely articulate it.

'Who are you? How come you look just like me? Balam Lehane is dead.'

'Too right, Balam's dead. I held that bum's head down in that cesspit 'till he wasn't wriggling no more. Can't have no . . . pretenders to the throne.'

'Tell me.' Abdon was transfixed.

'I'm your daddy, Abdon. Your real daddy.'

# CHAPTER 31

The stranger smiled contemptuously. It was a rotten grin besmirched by tobacco and liquor. Abdon did not share the burglar's humour. Indeed, Abdon shivered.

'I know what you're thinking, boy: he ain't old enough to be my daddy. Well, son, I was making babies when I was just a baby.'

This revelation was uncomfortable for Abdon, yet his loyalty was unshaken. He dared not look Fabian in the eye: this invader to his home, like a hungry wolf, had a sixth sense for danger. Nor would Fabian meet Abdon's eye. As Fabian continued his clandestine manipulations, Abdon could practically read Fabian's mind. Keep him distracted, Abdon.

'I don't understand.' Abdon feigned confusion. He had to keep the interloper talking.

'I'll tell you.' The killer's face radiated menacing glee.

The Olivers had been drifters and petty crooks. Since Laban had been a baby, all he had ever remembered was living on the run. Laban's father had always described himself as cursed. When there was no work in the fields, what choice did he have but to pick pockets or spirit away longhorns? A few idle rich would never miss a couple of bucks. Even then, the lawmen took exception. They'd let you off if you were a teenager who had never been in trouble. Why were they always after him? He was damned if he did, and damned if he didn't.

Laban, like his father and grandfather, had also inherited that distinctive crescent moon birthmark. Laban's father had always said that the Olivers had been born under a bad sign, and that blemish proved it. The unmistakeable disfigurement made it easy for witnesses to remember Mack Oliver. Thus, there had been a recurring event in Laban's childhood. There would be a knock on the door of whatever filthy hovel the Olivers were then behind with the rent on. Mack would answer and greet the lawman who was inevitably waiting outside. He had tangled with sheriffs so many times that Mack had long memorized an encyclopaedia of persuasive excuses. Mack's convincing protestations would keep them at bay for one more night.

As soon as Mack bid the marshal a cordial goodnight, the packing would begin in frenzy. The Olivers would be away in their pilfered covered wagon within hours. It would always be a long ride: the next county, or even the next state. Mack had learned that it was a small world, especially for a man with his unconventional looks. There had been occasions when Mack had been recognized in the next town and been compelled to flee once again. The secret to a successful escape, Mack had learned, was distance, distance, distance.

Nadine Oliver had had a touch of Lady Macbeth about her. Nadine and Mack had been common law spouses, Laban had overheard. Laban had not understood what that meant until adulthood. Lawless bum though his father had been, Mack had also been a clueless sap. His pathetic thefts and cons had seldom been his ideas. Nadine had manipulatively planted the seeds of ideas in Mack's head. Mack had always been so self-pitying and aggrieved at his lot that he had been easy to sway. It was one of Nadine's ideas that had turned Laban into an orphan.

Laban, as an only child, had very much been left to his own devices. He was occasionally a forced accomplice in his parents' crooked ploys, but for the most part he had been an afterthought. The Olivers had never realized how slyly intelligent their offspring was.

Laban had watched his parents' schemes with the detachment of an independent observer. He had learned what worked, and what did not. Laban, who had never spent a day in the schoolhouse, had also taught himself to read and write.

The boy had also become an accomplished burglar and housebreaker. Mack had sometimes brought Laban along if a particular window had been too small. When his parents were not looking (which was almost always), Laban would strike out on burglaries of his own. He had never been detected, though he had never thieved more than trinkets nor toys.

Laban did not know how old he was, but he guessed that he would have been around fifteen when his parents got themselves shot. The Olivers had learned that a rancher was keeping his payroll in the safe in his house. The ranch house had been large and well-appointed. Nadine and Mack would have to search the building together.

Laban had been a lookout that night. He had urged his parents to let him break in. Laban had divined a number of flaws in their ill-conceived plan – not least that the rancher would be at home in bed during the burglary. Mack had silenced his son with backhands, though. When Laban had heard the shotgun blasts and screams from within, he had sighed.

'Told you so,' he had moaned before heading straight for the covered wagon.

Laban had scratched out a living in the Oliver tradition, he was smarter than his folks. Laban would hold down a job busting sod or mucking out stables, and he would add to his earnings with prolific burglaries. By the time the local crime wave was so bad that attention turned to the stranger with the devil's fingerprint on his cheek, Laban had always vanished.

Laban would have continued, had he not fortuitously seen that newspaper article. The Bank of Bethesda had made a huge donation to their local church. There had been a photograph next to the article showing the bank's managers. The daguerreotype of Abdon had struck Laban. The photo had also inspired him.

Laban had had a number of trysts with local girls. He had inherited his father's glib charm, and his mother's cunning. With young women, Laban had expertly memorized the script. He vaguely remembered stopping in Bethesda for a while, though Laban had not recalled the girl in question. Both Laban and Mack had borne the disfigurement. With that birthmark, this Abdon Timpson had to be his kindred.

It was as if Laban was a loner who suddenly had a rapt audience. He did not seem to want to shut up.

'What if I could step into your shoes? I look just like you. Maybe I can take over the bank.'

Stunned, Abdon listened in silence. He was not certain

whether Laban was merely deluded, or dangerously brazen.

'Took some work. I had to check out what happened to the girl I lay with, and what happened to the babies. And some cleaning up. Can't have any awkward questions. The Lehanes, Calista Richards, Balam, those Poles – all out of the picture. You're next. After I get your papers.'

'Laban, are you certain this will work?' Abdon asked desperately. 'The staff at the bank. All our customers in town. They all know us. How will you get away with this?'

'Leave that to me, smart alec.' Laban in fact schemed to hide Abdon's body, steal the ownership papers, and sell up through an attorney in another town. It was a massive risk, Laban had calculated, but the payoff would be spectacular.

'Laban – do you know anything about antiquarian weapons?'

'What the. . . ?'

With unnatural calm, Fabian pulled back the lever of the Limey. He aimed the barrel, then pressed down on the trigger. The rifle thundered, and Laban collapsed bleeding in a sandstorm of black soot.

# CHAPTER 32

Abdon had feared how his parents would react to his return after his impulsive exit. He had also been desperate to save them from the unknown menace stalking Bethesda. Fabian and Ida, too, had worried that they had lost their precious child forever. All had seemed hopeless, and then Laban's menacing invasion had terrified them.

All these fears dissolved as the Timpsons, reunited, embraced. Ida's face still red from her tears, Abdon and Fabian still bruised from Laban's assaults, the three held each other close to their breasts. While the killer's dead body smouldered on the floor, the Timpsons chattered. It was as if Abdon had come home from a long vacation. Indeed, as he shared the results of what he called his 'investigation', Abdon spoke candidly and energetically. Though he inevitably had to describe the circumstances of his birth and adoption, Abdon talked without embarrassment nor hesitation. They were, after all, his parents. He could tell them anything.

The report of the Limey drew armed men to the house. Bethesdans looked after one another, and the Timpsons were highly respected. Fifield led the posse. He stormed in, terrified for his friends' safety, only to find Abdon oddly calm.

The Old Man had always been such a curmudgeon to him, but Abdon was moved to see Fifield. The bank manager was practically an uncle to him. Abdon rushed over to hug his old boss. Fifield, blushing despite himself, returned the embrace. The veteran had been insensible with worry during Abdon's exile.

'Abdon . . .' Fifield's voice was breaking. 'You're home! What the heck happened?'

'Well, Mr Fifield,' Abdon chirped. 'It all started . . .'

Abdon now had an excuse to describe his heroics all over again. Fifield normally found Abdon's boasts a little tiresome. Tonight, he was intrigued.

The posse, reassured that the Timpsons were safe, dragged Laban's smoky remains away. The Timpsons and Fifield, though they had every reason to be exhausted and emotional, chattered away until dawn. Ida fuelled them with cocoa and cornbread. His mother and father urged him to rest for a while. Abdon, though, insisted on returning to the bank on Monday. He longed for his old routine.

'It's been a shock for Mr Fifield, too,' Abdon piped. 'If he wants to take some time off, I'm sure I could be' – he coughed theatrically – 'an able substitute.'

They laughed. Abdon's perpetual self-regard – grating as it could be – was a sign of his well-being.

'Next week, though, I'd like to take the train back to Crosskeys.'

On Monday morning, Abdon felt like an Aztec mummy as he rose stiffly from his bed. His flesh had coloured from his violent encounters. Rings of purple, red and brown spotted his pale skin. Abdon thought his flesh resembled oily circles in a muddy puddle. His limbs and joints ached from the beatings he had received and delivered. He had to steel himself to dress and limp into town to the bank.

When he arrived, Abdon could not help but laugh. He had yet to open up, but the queue already stretched around the corner. Abdon rightly guessed that everybody would want an appointment today.

Indeed, the week of his homecoming came to be one of the happiest of his life. The perfect salesman, Abdon told his story over and over again. During meeting after meeting, Abdon turned his tale into profit. The bank's reserves swelled after deposit after deposit was credited. Abdon also set up a score of promising loans. He worked late every night, before joining Fifield and his parents for dinner. All they discussed was their future. They were already starting to forget Laban's hateful meddling.

Abdon had told Fabian about the Crosskeys work camp. His father had been touched by the support Lynch had given Abdon. Fabian had made inquiries, then arranged for Lynch to meet Abdon once more.

Saturday morning, Abdon returned to Crosskeys. As joyful and exciting as the week had been, he felt a little deflated during the train journey. Abdon did not feel as if he had lost a brother. His secret past had taught him that family meant so much more than blood. Fabian and Ida were his parents, and nothing would ever change that. With Balam, though, it was as if there was a friendship that had never come to be. It was too late for Balam, who had been drowned like a rat by his own father. Perhaps Abdon could help the surrogate brothers that had adopted Balam, though.

Abdon had also been reflecting on the nature of the men he had encountered. Balam, raised in a madhouse and unjustly imprisoned, had remained loyal and sanguine. Fabian was a retired gentleman banker. Yet, his father had bravely tricked Laban with a hazardous ploy. Smooth-talking Abdon, filled with indignant rage, had unleashed his anger on Halbert and Bennett.

Your schooling, wealth and privilege don't matter, Abdon had concluded. Nor does the brains, looks, or temperament you're born with. Each man makes his own decisions as to how he wants to live. Lynch was stony-faced as he greeted Abdon at the station. Inwardly, though, Lynch was glad to encounter the young man again. Lynch had heard what had happened in Bethesda. When they shook hands, Lynch was pleased to see Abdon intact.

'Welcome back, Abdon. How can I help? Do you need to ride out to the camp again?'

'In a little while, partner. First, let me talk about how I can help you.'

Abdon led Lynch to a café. Lynch could scarcely believe what he was hearing when Abdon discussed acting as a trustee for his work programme. Perhaps he could even help to find the reformed prisoners jobs in Bethesda. Abdon could talk the talk well enough, Lynch mused. Is he serious, though?

Abdon slid a cheque over the table to Lynch: a donation from the Bank of Bethesda. This generosity could pay for a lot of equipment, wages and food. Abdon was matching his bluster with cash.

'In return, Mr Lynch, I'd like a newspaper to come and cover our partnership. With a photograph. This is darn good publicity for the bank.'

Abdon smiled arrogantly, but he was very difficult to dislike. If he and Abdon were going to be working together, Lynch concluded, he would have to put up with his vanity.

'Going to get you good today, Halbert,' hissed Bennett. 'Real good.'

Bennett's fists squeezed the bars between his cell and Halbert's. His face, already skeletal, became more distorted when he pushed it against the metal rods. Bennett could easily reach through the bars and claw at Halbert. Sometimes he did, and Halbert flinched from Bennett's touch.

Halbert retreated to the back wall of the chamber. He thought that he was stoically disregarding Bennett's taunts with stony silence. Halbert's flickering eyes and trembling lips exposed his inner whimpering, though. He had always told himself that he was a tough guy, even when pushing around somebody much weaker than himself. Halbert had often gloated about the unfortunates he had beaten up. In Blackmill, though, he was the unfortunate.

The other prisoners were train robbers, gunmen, or whatever the heck Bennett was. They could sense Halbert's terrified vulnerability. Before being locked up, Halbert had mocked tattletales that went squealing to the sheriff. Inside, Halbert never strayed far from the guards' protective eyes. He volunteered for any work detail or dirty job. Halbert would do anything to get away from the other prisoners. Indeed, the inmates called him Blackmill's number one butt kisser.

He was nearly there, though. The end of his sentence was in sight.

After Abdon sprained Halbert's wrist, Halbert had headed straight for the nearest whiskey hole. There, Halbert had drunkenly shared his own falsified explanation of his fight with Abdon. Nobody had believed him. Their scorn had inspired him to drink even more. The liquor had numbed the pain in his joint. Within hours, Halbert had been brawling once again.

This time, he had not been permitted to sleep it off in jail. Halbert's rap sheet was prolific, yet pathetic: fights, public drunkenness, shoplifting cans of beans. Halbert's brother had sworn to the circuit judge that Halbert had great remorse and great potential. The justice had not been impressed.

'This time, I will not let you off with a fine. Six months in Blackmill will straighten you out.'

Despite himself, Halbert now agreed with the judge. There was no way in heck that he was ever returning here.

The bars of the cage vibrated as the turnkey's nightstick clanged on the metal.

'Get back, Bennett,' barked the guard. 'You – Halbert. Get over here. Visitors.'

Making a show of his deference and respect, Halbert rushed over to the cell door.

'Right away, sir,' he cheeped. Halbert always stressed his cheerful obedience around the prison officers. Inwardly, though, he was uneasy. In three months, nobody had ever come to see him. Halbert's only family was his brother. Even he, Halbert suspected, was washing his hands of Halbert.

The guard unlocked Halbert's cell and led him along the landing. As he passed Bennett's cell, Halbert tried to ignore the obscenities Bennett cackled. Instinctively, though, Halbert's eyes darted sideways in fear as he walked past Bennett.

The turnkey led Halbert up to the warden's office. Halbert gulped as he entered. 'Why am I being taken to the warden's office?' he wondered.

Within, standing alongside the warden, were three other men. Two were strangers: a stony-faced, burly figure and a redhead with blazing eyes. The other man was Abdon Timpson, unforgettable with his unique birthmark.

'Halbert,' the warden began. 'You've been a good prisoner. I was contemplating your early release, when these visitors came along.'

Halbert felt nauseous. He had been praying for the end of this ordeal, promising the guards that he was a reformed man. What lies, or truths, had that brat been whispering in the warden's ear?

'Didn't recognize you, Halbert. You've lost weight,' said Abdon with matter-of-factness. Indeed, Halbert had grown very thin. Blackmill hardly indulged its guests. Moreover, the larger, stronger prisoners often stole Halbert's meals.

'Yes, sir,' Halbert agreed. He was not quite as chirpy now.

Abdon approached Halbert, holding his face as close to the prisoner's as possible. Halbert was edgy, and Abdon was enjoying this reaction.

'Early release?' Abdon continued. 'I came here today to make sure you got what you deserved.'

Halbert swallowed so nervously that he had to shut his eyes.

'Halbert – would you like a job?'